The Babbs Switch Story

Also by Darleen Bailey Beard

The Flimflam Man

a chapter book with pictures by Eileen Christelow

Twister

a picture book illustrated by Nancy Carpenter

Darleen Bailey Beard

The
Babbs
Switch
Story

FARRAR STRAUS GIROUX   NEW YORK

www.fsgkidsbooks.com

Library of Congress Cataloging-in-Publication Data
Beard, Darleen Bailey.
    The Babbs Switch story / Darleen Bailey Beard.— 1st ed.
        p. cm.
    Summary: In 1924, twelve-year-old Ruthie finds her life in a small Oklahoma
town complicated by the behavior of her older sister Daphne, an object of ridicule
and dislike because of her limited mental abilities.
    ISBN-13: 978-0-374-30475-1
    ISBN-10: 0-374-30475-0
    [1. Mentally handicapped—Fiction.   2. Sisters—Fiction.   3. Oklahoma—
Fiction.]   I. Title.

PZ7.B374 Bab 2002
[Fic]—dc21

                                                        2001033337

This book is dedicated to my sister, Sherrie Lee Bailey Koger. When we were children, Sherrie would wink at me. I'd spend the rest of the day trying to get her to look at me so I could wink back. Well, this book serves as the wink-of-all-winks. I love you, sister, Tag-Along Bailey.

Acknowledgments

Many thanks to the kind volunteers at the Kiowa County Historical Museum, in Hobart, Oklahoma, for sharing their valuable time, knowledge, newspaper articles, photographs, phone calls, and faxes: Wilma Reneau, Harriet Stockton, Jessie Pyron, Bertha Ellis, Paul and Lucy Bieberdorf, Nona Bell Funkhouser, Bonnie Lenz, Jewell Pankhurst, Cecil Pankhurst and Mabel Pankhurst (both of whom sadly passed away before this book was completed), Robert Ferrell, and Wilma Campbell. Special thanks to Delbert Braun and Bill Williams, whose determination and love of history made the Kiowa County Historical Museum a reality; to Teddy and Wendy Block, museum curators; to Bill Braun, president of the Kiowa County Historical Society; and to Jerri Menz and Linda Branam of the Hobart Public Library. And finally, thanks to my grandmother, Oraleah Ferrier Bailey, who told me the Babbs Switch story when I was just a little girl.

The Babbs Switch Story

1

"What's that lump in your pillow?"

"Lump. Lump."

"Daphne Sue? Let me see."

Daphne folded the open end of her rose-embroidered pillowcase so I couldn't see inside. Then she turned, pulled something out, and rubbed it against her cheek.

Yawning, I opened my eyes in the early morning sun. Then I heard it, a faint meow.

"It's a kitten! You've got one of Daisy's kittens!" I jumped from bed, remembering the last time she had got ahold of Daisy's kittens. It was six months ago, on my twelfth birthday. I had to bury all five of them back behind the barn.

"My kitty!" Daphne held the kitten upside down, still rubbing it against her cheek. It was Boots, the little black one with white mittens and a mustache. "My kitty!"

"No. It's *not* yours. Now give it to me before you—"

She ran into our closet and scooted behind the dresses. "Mean Ruthie!"

"I am *not* mean. Now give me that kitten, or I'm telling Mom and Pop!"

Daphne didn't budge.

I reached behind the dresses, feeling for the kitten. Daphne's fingers were around his neck. "Daphne Sue! Stop squeezing him!" I pried her hands away, but it was too late. Boots flopped onto the floor, dead.

"You've killed him!" I grabbed his tiny body and held him to my nightgown.

The dresses parted, and out stepped Daphne. "Soft. Soft kitty." I could tell by her smile, she thought this was a fun game, and she tried to pull Boots from my hands.

"Stop it, Daphne. You've killed him."

Daphne placed her cheek on his dead body. "Soft. Soft. Love."

"Stop!" I pushed her face away. A lump swelled in my throat. "Where are the other two kittens?"

She covered her head with her pillow.

I looked around the room, in our dresser, under the pile of dirty clothes in the corner. Then I saw a lump under our quilt at the foot of our bed, and my heart started pounding.

Throwing back the quilt, I sighed. It was only the brick Mom heated every night and put in our bed to keep our feet warm.

My heart was pounding so loudly, I just knew Mom and

Pop would hear it and come running in from the kitchen. But they didn't.

"Daphne? I'm going to ask you one more time. Where are the other two kittens?"

Smiling, she pointed to the window.

"Are they outside? In the barn?"

She covered her eyes, squealing, "Peek-a-boo!"

I ran through the kitchen, in no mood for games. I yanked on my woolen wrap, then stormed outside, letting the screen door bump behind me.

Gusts of December wind slapped my face as I followed Daphne's helter-skelter tracks through the knee-deep snow, past our Tin Lizzy, around the chicken coop, to the barn. The door was standing wide open.

Surely she didn't kill the rest of Daisy's kittens. Please, God. Not like last time.

Smells of sweet corn and manure filled my nose. Cracks of sunlight squeezed between the boards, making stripes on the hay-covered floor and on Molly, our brown cow.

I ran to the far north corner, where an upside-down wheelbarrow served as a makeshift hidey-hole for Daisy and her babies. One end was propped up with a brick so Daisy could come and go—but the brick had been tossed aside.

I lifted the wheelbarrow right side up, afraid to breathe, afraid to look. *Please, God. Let them be alive.*

There, on one of my old flannel nightgowns as if nothing had happened, were Daisy and the other two kittens.

"Cinnamon! Nutmeg! Thank God you're safe!"

5

Daisy squinted as the morning sun filled her dark nest. She arched her back, stretching and yawning.

"I'm so sorry, Daisy." Tears dropped from my cheeks onto her head. "It's all my fault. I should have hidden you and your babies in the hayloft."

Daisy nudged her nose into my hands and purred.

"Boots is dead," I told her. And I knew she didn't understand the meaning of death any more than my sixteen-year-old sister, Daphne Sue, did.

2

"She's killed Boots."

Mom gasped.

Pop looked up from his oatmeal. "Daphne Sue? You know better than that."

But we all knew she didn't. She had an uncontrollable passion for soft things that even doctors couldn't explain. To her, a kitten was no different from my cotton leggings, Pop's goatskin gloves, or Mom's silk slip. If it was soft, she'd carry it around and rub it against her cheek. Sometimes, if she had something she wasn't supposed to have, she'd hide behind the sofa, in the chicken coop, or even in the outhouse.

"My kitty!" Daphne threw her bacon on the linoleum floor.

"Those kitties are *not* yours." Mom wiped Daphne's fingers with the washrag she kept close by. "You were a naughty little girl."

Daphne shook her head. "Big girl. Big girl."

Daphne was right. She *was* a big girl. A whole foot taller than me, with curves in places I only dreamed of.

Pop slurped long and loud on his cowpoke coffee. Cowpoke coffee was his specialty. He brewed it every morning with eggshells, vanilla, sugar, and milk. He'd let it sit all day long on the back of the cookstove, getting thicker and stronger by the minute. Sometimes, over the day, he'd add another eggshell or a spoon of molasses. Once, I caught him adding ketchup.

"Ruthie bird?" he said. "What about the others? Did she get them, too?"

"No," I said, shooting Daphne an angry look. "I hid them in the h-a-y-l-o-f-t."

Daphne threw another piece of bacon, and I knew it was because I'd spelled out a word. She always hated our doing that, since she didn't know how to spell.

"Looks like we got another two or three inches," Pop said, gazing out the window. "Must be a foot deep out there. I'll be darned if this isn't the biggest snowfall I've ever seen."

"Darned. Darned."

"Shh," Mom said, elbowing Pop. "See what you started?"

Pop smiled. "So where'd you put Boots?"

"In one of Molly's f-e-e-d s-a-c-k-s. I'm going to bury him before I go to school."

"Well, you better get a move on. You haven't much time. It'll take you a good half-hour just to walk to school in all this snow." Mom motioned to my plate. "Eat."

How can I think of food at a time like this? I took a bite, just to make Mom happy, then jumped into my brown tweed dress and woolen leggings, being sure to line my boots with newspaper to keep my feet warm.

I meandered into Mom's room, looking for something to bury Boots in. "Mom? Can I use this hatbox?" It was round and rose-colored, with a silk rope handle, sitting on top of Mom's dresser and holding bottles of perfume.

Mom shook her head.

"Please? It smells so nice, and it's the perfect size."

Mom raised an eyebrow.

"Please?"

"Well, all right." Mom was always careful with her hat-boxes. She didn't have very many, and what she did have she put to good use storing letters from all the relatives and spools of thread.

Mom grabbed the brush and braided my hair in two long tails. She tied the ends with the same brown ribbons they'd been tied with for as long as I could remember. "There you go," she said. "Brown is such a sensible color."

When I stepped outside and out of sight, I yanked off the ribbons. Brown might be sensible, but it sure was boring. Why wear plain brown when there were so many other dandy colors, like lemon yellow, sky blue, or apple green?

I lifted Boots out of Molly's feed sack and laid his lifeless body in the hatbox.

The ground was so frozen everywhere I tried to dig, the shovel would only go in about an inch. Finally, I settled on a spot at the edge of our cornfield where the soil had been tilled and was softer than the rest.

I dug deep, making sure the hatbox would fit. Opening the lid, I took one more look and traced Boots's white mustache and itty-bitty ear with my finger.

"Daphne didn't mean to kill you, Boots. Really, she didn't. You've got to understand, she's not right in the head. Folks in town say she's plumb crazy and shouldn't be allowed to live around decent, God-fearing Christians. But they don't know her the way we do. She's really not that bad, leastways if you're not a kitten."

Closing the lid, I lowered the hatbox into the ground and covered it with dirty snow and soil. I broke a stick in half and made a tiny cross for the grave.

Daisy stepped out of the barn and rubbed against my legs, meowing and sniffing the air. I picked her up and held her close.

Dear God,

Please let Boots go to the place where all good kittens go. And don't let any dogs dig him up before he gets there. Amen. Um, one more thing. Do You think You could help me keep an eye on Cinnamon and Nutmeg? I know You're awful busy helping old maids like Miss

Willowbright who's all crippled up with arthritis and bursitis and God only knows what else. I mean, um, You only know what else. But if these kittens are going to live to see the light of day, You'll have to keep Daphne's grubby paws off them. Amen.

3

"Guess how *Webster's Dictionary* defines *burp*?"

I didn't have to turn around to know who was speaking. I could tell by the hot breath on my neck. It was Elden Larrs, the most disgusting boy in School District 42.

"I *said*, Guess how *Webster's Dictionary* defines *burp*?"

I twirled my hair around and around my finger, feigning a sudden interest in Miss Holman's lesson on the Battle of Bunker Hill. But I knew he'd tell me, anyway.

" 'To eject wind noisily from the stomach through the mouth.' "

I turned around in my seat and stared my coldest stare. "Elden Larrs, you're sick."

"Thank you." He smiled, showing the chip in his front tooth from the time he jumped off the schoolhouse roof.

I scrunched my nose at him.

"Just admit it," Elden said, lifting my chin with his finger. "You're crazy-mad-in-love with me, Ruth Ann Tillman, and you know it."

"I'd sooner be in love with a frog."

"Would you kiss me if I were a frog?" He pretended to catch a fly with his tongue. "I might turn into Prince Charming."

"You? Prince Charming?" I covered my laugh.

He crossed his arms. "So how's Ding-Dong Daffy doing?"

"Her name is Daphne, and you know it," I said, facing forward again.

"Daffy, Daphne. What's the difference?"

"Mr. Larrs?" Miss Holman said. "Would you care to stand and finish this lesson?"

"No, ma'am."

"Then please be quiet and stop bothering your neighbors."

I wanted to snicker and say, "Ha! Serves you right!," but I didn't.

"And so Colonel Prescott issued his famous order, 'Don't one of you fire until you can see the whites of their eyes.' The Americans allowed the British to advance almost to the base of the earthworks and then surprised them with open fire."

"Is *vomit* spelled with an *e* or an *i*?"

I turned back around. "Give me that dictionary! If you'd quit looking up every revolting word you can think of and start listening, you might accidentally learn something."

13

Elden smiled. "I'm learnin'. I'm learnin'. I just learned somethin' that *you* probably don't know."

"What?"

"Not gonna tell you."

"Good. I don't want to know."

"Yeah, you do."

"No, I don't."

"Then I'll tell you, anyway." He leaned up close. "*Earwax* is one word, not two."

"Elden Larrs! When I get rich and famous and write my autobiography, I'm going to tell the whole world how positively absolutely disgusting you are."

"Oh yeah?" He squared his chin. "How the heck are *you* gonna get rich and famous?"

"As a singer, naturally. I'm going to be the next Bessie Smith, Empress of the Blues."

"I wouldn't count on it."

"Why not?"

" 'Cause you can't sing worth a lick."

"I can, too, and you know it. You're just jealous."

"Me? Jealous?"

"Just wait until Miss Holman announces the parts for our Christmas Tree Celebration. I'll be the soloist. You'll see."

Elden couldn't argue much about that. I'd sung the solo in our Christmas Tree Celebration for the last three years. Folks were always telling me that I sang like a canary. And Pop said I sang before I learned to talk, which is why he called me Ruthie bird.

I crossed my eyes at Elden. "Someday you're going to hear me on the radio."

"Radio! That's a hoot. We ain't got electricity in Babbs Switch, Oklahoma."

"Well, Hobart has electricity. Miss Holman says one day electricity will be as common as cows!"

"Then Miss Holman don't know nothin'."

I turned back around in my chair. That Elden Larrs made as much sense as a two-headed mule with half a brain.

4

Everyone took turns jabbing a piping-hot baked potato from the five-gallon coffee tin. They had been baking all morning long inside our coal stove, tempting our tummies with their earthy aroma.

Small curls of steam rose into the air as we split open their white bellies.

"One dollop each," Miss Holman said, guarding the crock of sweet cream butter.

Yellow butter melted onto my potato like drops of golden sunshine. Then I took my usual seat next to Violet on the corner of the stage.

"Well, are you excited?" she asked.

"About what?"

"About the Christmas Tree Celebration!" She rolled her eyes as if I should have read her mind. Mashing her potato with a fork, she continued, "Miss Holman's going to announce our parts after lunch. I'll just die if I don't get to be a dancing snowflake. Do you think I'll get the part?"

For the last two weeks, Violet had pranced and waved and fluttered so much, I was ready to proclaim her Queen of the Dancing Snowflakes. If she didn't get the part, *I* would die, because I'd never hear the end of it.

"You'll be a dancing snowflake, Vi."

"I hope. Everyone already knows *you'll* get the solo."

"Everyone but Elden. He says I can't sing worth a lick."

Violet stuffed a forkful of potato into her mouth. "Don't pay any attention to that flat tire."

I took a bite of my potato.

"So, how are the kittens? Have they opened their eyes yet?"

I put down my fork. My eyes filled with tears. "Oh, Vi. Something awful happened."

Violet stopped chewing, and butter ran down her chin. "Did Daphne get ahold of them?"

"Just one."

"Which one?"

"Boots."

"She didn't, you know—"

I nodded.

"Oh, nuts! What did you do?"

"I hid Cinnamon and Nutmeg in the hayloft, and I buried Boots at the edge of the cornfield."

"Don't worry, Ruthie. When the weather warms up, we'll give Boots a proper funeral."

"We will?"

"Sure we will. You can be the preacher and say nice things about him. You know, quote some Scripture and look real serious. I'll bring some of my mom's daffodils and my harmonica. I'm real good at 'Heaven's Doors Are Opening.' I played it when my cousin's dog, Little Flea Bag, got run over by a hay baler."

"Your cousin has a dog named Little Flea Bag?"

"*Had* a dog named Little Flea Bag. She was a Doberman pinscher."

"A Doberman pinscher? That's not a little dog."

"She was when they first got her." Violet smiled and held out her pinky. "Friends till the cow jumps over the moon?"

"And the dish runs away with the spoon!"

Then we locked pinkies for the millionth time.

5

"Class, I have some important announcements," Miss Holman said. We had all lined up to scrub our forks and plates in the bucket of warm water that one of the boys had brought up from the cistern. "First, Elden's baby sister, Elizabeth, is going to play the part of Jesus in our Christmas Tree Celebration."

Everyone clapped.

Elden took a bow, plopping his fork into the bucket.

Little Howard Sulkey raised his hand. He was always raising his hand for one reason or another. And the bad thing was, he didn't raise it nice and quiet, the way everybody else did. Instead, he had to moan and groan like a sick cow. Most of the kids thought it was funny, especially the boys, but I was about ready to put a cork in his mouth.

"Eww. Ewwww!"

"Yes, Howard?"

"Isn't Baby Jesus supposed to be a boy?"

"Yes," Miss Holman said. "But no one in Babbs Switch *has* a baby boy. Besides, the audience won't know; she'll be wrapped in a white towel."

Elden took another bow, this time dropping his plate into the bucket, splashing water onto the floor. "If it weren't for Elizabeth, we'd have to use a dumb ol' doll like last year. Remember?"

Everyone laughed. How could we *forget?* We'd used a doll that belonged to Maybelle. For some reason, its head wouldn't stay on, and when the Virgin Mary picked up Baby Jesus, his head fell off and rolled across the stage. The audience roared with laughter. The Virgin Mary forgot her lines and bumped into the scenery. It was all downhill from there.

Miss Holman pulled out a sheet of paper. "When you all stop laughing and sit down, I'll announce the parts for our celebration."

We zipped through the line, scrubbing our plates and forks and drying them on the big dish towel.

It took us a while to quiet down. Elden kept making catcalls and meowing at Maybelle Smith, who had a secret crush on him, only it wasn't very secret because everybody knew, including Elden.

Violet and I locked pinkies long distance.

When there wasn't a single speck of noise, Miss Holman put on her glasses. "The Three Wise Men will be—R. W. McBee, Howard Sulkey, and Elden Larrs."

I looked at Violet. *Elden Larrs? A wise man? God help us.*

Miss Holman continued. "Our soloist will be—Ruth Ann Tillman."

My insides jumped. I gave Violet a smile, then turned to look at Mr. Smartypants. "See? I told you."

"So? I'm a wise man."

"Very funny. Ha-ha."

Miss Holman continued, assigning parts for the Virgin Mary, Joseph, the sheep, the camel, the star of Bethlehem, Santa Claus, the narrator, the curtain puller-upper, and the stage clean-up crew.

"Last but not least, our dancing snowflakes will be— Ruby Tallchief and Clyde Bushyhead. And our donkey will be—Violet Kline."

I gasped. Poor Vi! I tried to get her to look my way, but she drooped in her desk like week-old lettuce.

"I also want to remind you that next Wednesday is our first rehearsal. I expect everyone to be here. Fix-Up Day is a week from Saturday." Miss Holman motioned around the room. "We've finally got the school board's approval to paint the inside *and* outside of the building. And Clayton Rader's mother is going to donate fresh spruce trimmings to drape around the windows."

None of us liked the school board's decision to nail steel netting over all the windows to keep out vandals. So far, though, it had worked: no more coal had been stolen. But the steel netting let in hardly any light, making our one-room schoolhouse dark as a dungeon. And I hated that even though the windows could open, we couldn't get out. Not that we went around jumping from windows—except for maybe Elden—but if something happened and we needed to get out in a hurry, we couldn't.

"Tell your mothers to bring a potluck dish and your fathers to bring turpentine and brushes. The school board is providing the paint."

"Eww! Ewwww!"

"Yes, Howard?"

"Isn't it dangerous to bring turpentine? My pappy says this schoolhouse is so old and weathered, it's like a matchbox waitin' to catch fire."

Miss Holman tightened her lips. I could tell she didn't like Howard any more than the rest of us did. And it wasn't just his constant moaning and groaning, but the way he always acted so high-and-mighty, as if he knew more than the rest of us, even Miss Holman. 'Course, that probably was because his ma always called him her "little genius" in front of everybody.

"Don't worry, Howard. We'll be extra careful with the turpentine."

"Are we gonna have real costumes?" Clyde Bushyhead asked.

"You mean *going* to have real costumes," she corrected.

Clyde blushed.

"Yes. On Monday the ladies from the Quartz Mountain Sewing Circle are coming to measure everyone."

Smiles filled the room, except from Violet. She was still wilting.

"You mean we don't have to wear those ugly old sheets and towels like last year?" R. W. McBee asked.

Miss Holman smiled. "Thanks to our fall bake sale, we earned enough money to buy several bolts of material. R.W., since you're one of the wise men, you get to wear royal purple and red."

"What about me?" Maybelle asked.

"Eww. Ewww. Do I have to wear purple and red?"

Miss Holman went down her list, telling all the kids what color they would wear. When she came to me, I thought I'd died and gone to heaven: "The soloist gets to wear blue velvet with silver ribbons in her hair."

Blue velvet? Silver ribbons? I fingered the ugly brown ribbons in my pocket, the same ugly brown ribbons I'd tried to hide for years. A smile trickled all the way down to my toes. *This is going to be the best Christmas Tree Celebration ever!*

6

"Do I look like a donkey?"

Poor Vi. Her neck was all red and blotchy, the way it always gets when she's upset.

"Well? Do I?"

"Of course not. You look more like a dancing snowflake."

"Exactly. I *am* a dancing snowflake. I'm not a donkey. I didn't even try *out* for the donkey."

"I know, Vi." I linked my arm through hers as we walked down the railroad tracks. "Maybe being a dancing snowflake isn't all it's cracked up to be. I mean, with all that prancing and fluttering and stuff."

Violet stopped walking. "A dancing snowflake is the most important part in the play. It's even more important than soloist. It takes a lot of timing and precision. Not everybody can prance and twirl and flutter the way I can, you know."

I nodded. "What if you get dizzy or something? What if

you throw up on the stage, right there in front of everybody? If you ask me, you're better off playing the donkey."

"That's easy for *you* to say, Miss Soloist. Besides, who asked you?"

"You did."

Violet unlinked her arm from mine and walked a little faster. "Well, I didn't ask for *that*."

"Vi, I'm just trying to help. All I'm saying is maybe you'll *like* playing the donkey. Give it a try."

"Never!" Violet held her arms high. She pranced down the tracks, fluttering her fingers and letting them fall gently like drops of snow. "See? I can dance circles around Clyde Bushyhead. He's about as graceful as an ox! And Ruby Tallchief couldn't dance her way out of a gunnysack!"

Violet was right. Ruby Tallchief was nearsighted something awful and refused to wear her glasses because Maybelle had said, "Looky, snooky, here comes Booky!" the very first time Ruby had worn them.

"If you ask me, Elden should've gotten the part of the donkey. He doesn't even need a costume," I said.

Violet finally broke a smile, and we laughed all the way from Ol' Man Rhemmer's haystack to the empty boxcar that served as the official Babbs Switch train depot. The depot was the halfway point between her house and mine, and we often stopped there to warm up. In the springtime, we would fill our pockets with the wild blueberries that grew by the tracks, or pick honeysuckle and suck out all the honey. Sometimes we didn't have any reason for stopping, so we'd just hang around and watch the four o'clock Rock Island go by, waving at all the hoboes and making up tragic stories about their lives.

We slid open the depot door, letting sunshine spill inside.

"Do you think Miss Holman made a mistake?" Violet's voice echoed in the boxcar. "It would be easy to do, you know. Maybe she meant Clyde would be the donkey, and Ruby and I would be dancing snowflakes."

"Ask her." Poor Vi. She was really getting desperate.

"You're right." Violet had a new, determined look in her eye. "Tomorrow I'll just ask her point-blank, 'Did you make a mistake?' And she'll apologize and get it all straightened out. That's what this is, just a big mistake."

"That's right," I agreed. But she knew as well as I did that Miss Holman never made mistakes.

7

I slip-slid across the empty parking lot of Tillman's Mercantile, the store my parents owned. But when I got to the door, I stopped cold in my tracks.

Usually, our mercantile was the hub of Babbs Switch. Folks were always coming and going, picking up their mail, exchanging the latest goings-on, or buying supplies. It was nothing to see a good three or four buggies and a couple of autos parked out front. But today there were no autos. No buggies. No one hauling gasoline in five-gallon cans.

The sign on the door said CLOSED.

The only time I remembered Mom and Pop closing during the day was when Grandma had died two summers ago. A lump jumped into my throat.

With one eye shut, I peeked between the butcher-paper advertisements on the front window. Right between *"Sliced*

Beef 23 cents per pound" and "Milk 15 cents per gallon," I saw Mom and Pop, crying something awful.

I stood there watching, feeling kind of guilty, as if I was seeing something I shouldn't. I'd never seen my parents cry before, not much, anyway.

Mom cried now and then, especially when she got letters from her twin sister, Harriett Sue. And Pop cried the time he dropped the cash register on his big toe, but I could tell this was something more serious.

Their eyes were all red and puffy, as if they'd been crying for a long time. For a minute I wanted to run—run to the depot and pretend I'd never seen their tears. Then I swallowed hard and jiggled the doorknob.

Mom and Pop looked up, surprised.

"Well . . . there's my Ruthie bird!" Pop said, forcing a smile. "Um, er, did you notice we closed early today?"

"Yes." My own eyes welled with tears. "What's wrong?"

Mom finger-combed her hair. She made herself smile, too. "Nothing's wrong, Ruthie. We just decided to take the rest of the day off. That's all."

I put my books on the counter, twirling an ornery strand of hair round and round. "So why are you both crying?"

"Crying? Um . . . well, funny thing—" Pop began.

"It's a long story," Mom interrupted. "Too long to tell. You understand."

How could I? The lump in my throat grew. "Is it Grandpa?"

"Oh no, Ruthie bird," Pop said. "It's nothing like that."

I sighed, then remembered the kittens. "It's the kittens, isn't it? Did Daphne get them?"

Mom and Pop looked at each other, then at me. "No," said Pop. "She didn't get the kittens."

"Then what is it? Why are you both crying, and why is the store closed? You *never* close the store early."

They didn't answer.

I stood my ground. "Mom? Pop?"

"Ruthie, do your chores," said Mom.

"But—"

"Chores!"

I grabbed the broom. *I'll never understand parents.* Swish. *At least there's one way to find out what's going on around here.* Swish. *Good old-fashioned eavesdropping.* Swish. *Tonight.*

8

I lay in bed, listening to Mom and Pop's low voices and the tinkling of spoons at the kitchen table. Daphne was lying next to me, holding Josephine, her one-armed, bald-headed rag doll.

". . . fifty-eight, fifty-nine, *sixty*!" Josephine's only hand touched each square of our quilt, as it had done every night for as far back as I could remember—and I could remember when Josephine had two arms and long red pigtails.

None of us could figure out why Daphne was good at counting. She couldn't spell. She couldn't read. She couldn't even sing the alphabet without skipping *l m n o p*. But she could count like nobody's business, and she did it everywhere she went—at church, at the Kiowa Theater, at taffy pulls, at picnics. She never got tired of counting the same things over and over.

That was how I knew there were sixty squares in our

quilt, one hundred forty-nine panels of wood in our bed-room ceiling, and ninety-eight pickets in our white picket fence.

Every Sunday we knew exactly how many folks came to church, something Pastor BoJo came to rely on when he shook hands after the sermon. "So, how many folks attended this morning, Daphne Sue?" he'd ask. If Daphne said one or two more than last week, Pastor BoJo would smile and look right pleased. He was always saying we'd have a special service the day we hit fifty.

Usually, there were thirty-seven or thirty-nine, depending on whether Mrs. Rutledge brought her grown sons, Hank and Hal. They were plumb past the age of marrying, a good twenty or twenty-one at least, and they were lazy as all get-out. Rumor had it they were as useless as a blister on their mama's behind.

Daphne even tried to count the money when Pastor BoJo passed the offering plate. Once, she picked up a nickel and had a hissy fit when Pop pried it from her fingers and made her drop it back into the plate.

Daphne jumped up and down on the bed. She tucked her flannel gown into the waistband of her underpants and held up her arm like the Statue of Liberty.

"Daphne Sue, will you please stop that?"

"Soft kitty kitty." Daphne stomped her foot. "Tell kitties."

"Promise you'll quit jumping?"

Daphne plopped down, rattling the bedsprings, and

pulled her nightgown around her knees. "Tell kitties. Soft. Love."

"Daisy has two kittens." I choked on the number two.

"Green?"

"No, goose egg. Kittens don't come in green."

"Green!" Daphne insisted.

"Cinnamon is orange. Nutmeg is gray."

"Boots?"

I bit my lip. "Boots was black-and-white."

Daphne squeezed my hand. "Soft? Soft?"

"Yes. Very soft." I stretched my toes down to the hot brick that warmed our bed.

"Hold?"

"No."

"Hold!"

"No. Now go to sleep!" I rolled over and faced the wall. Just the thought of Daphne getting her grubby paws around one more kitten's neck made me want to clobber her.

"Can't sleep."

"Daphne Sue, you promised."

"Kiss?"

"Oh, all right." I rolled over and kissed her on the cheek.

"Kiss."

I kissed her other cheek.

"Kiss."

I kissed her forehead.

She held up Josephine, and I knew what she wanted. "Don't even ask."

"Kiss?"

"If you'd let Mom wash that dumb doll once in a while, she wouldn't smell to high heaven."

"No smell. No smell."

"She does *too* smell. Just like stinky feet!"

Daphne pushed Josephine into my face.

"Stop." But I knew if I didn't kiss her stupid rag doll, she'd keep me up all night. Then I wouldn't get to eavesdrop on Mom and Pop in the kitchen. So I held my nose and gave Josephine a quick, kinda-sorta, halfway kiss.

9

When Daphne's breathing finally slowed, I crept out of bed, tiptoed across the shadowy room, and stood behind our door, listening to the kitchen voices.

"I should have kept a better eye on her," Mom said. "I should have known something like this could happen."

I stepped closer, twirling my hair.

"We *both* should have known," Pop said.

Should have known what?

A chair scooted.

Coffee poured into cups.

Spoons clinked.

"Do you think Mrs. Larrs will tell anyone?" Mom asked.

Needle-nose Larrs? Elden's mother? I stepped into the hall, over the floorboard that always creaked, and pressed my ear against the wall.

"Knowing Mrs. Larrs, she probably will," Pop replied.

"She kept screaming, 'Daphne's smothering my baby! Daphne's smothering my baby!' I couldn't calm her down."

Smothering her baby? Daphne? A chill went down my arms.

"You know how Daphne loves soft things," Pop said. "She was probably trying to take the baby's blanket, and Elizabeth got tangled up in it. That's all."

"I know that. You know that. But Mrs. Larrs doesn't know that."

"Thank the Lord, Elizabeth let out a good, loud scream," Pop said. "You know, I'm surprised Daphne would even get close to Elizabeth, after what happened last Sunday in church service."

"I know," Mom replied.

I remembered last Sunday. Pastor BoJo had just started preaching about hellfire and damnation when baby Elizabeth let out one of her bloodcurdling screams. She screamed and screamed as if someone had stuck her with a pin.

Daphne couldn't stand the screaming, so she covered her ears and crawled under the pew. I thought Pop was going to have to pry her out with a crowbar.

"What would we have done if Elizabeth hadn't screamed?"

"Shh," Mom said. "It's too dreadful to imagine."

I twirled my hair faster and faster, clear to the scalp, then back the other way.

Mom's voice grew angry and loud. "Lord knows, I've raised Daphne in a good Christian home. I've tried doctors, medicines, hospitals. You name it, I've tried it. And now this. When's it going to end, Larry? That's what I want to know."

"It may never end. But we've got to keep the faith."

"Keep the faith? I'm so weary, I haven't any faith to keep!"

"Ella Bess, you don't mean that."

"I *do* mean that. Right now I don't even believe there *is* a God."

No God? I dashed back to bed and covered my head.

Dear God,

I hope you didn't hear what Mom just said. But in case you did, she didn't really mean it. And I'm sure Daphne didn't mean what happened today, either. You know she wouldn't try to smother Elizabeth on purpose, don't you? Please help little Elizabeth to be all right. Amen.

I pulled the quilt back down around my neck. Daphne was snoring like a lumberjack, in long, even strokes.

The grandfather clock in the hall chimed eleven o'clock. Between the clock's chiming, Daphne's snoring, and my thoughts racing, I couldn't sleep a wink.

One more thing, God. Do you think you could make me good and sick tomorrow? It's not that I don't want

*to go to school. It's just that knowing how Needle-nose
Larrs likes to stick her nose in other people's business,
she's probably blabbed what happened to everybody
who's anybody, making a mountain out of a molehill.
Chicken pox would be dandy. Or even poison ivy.*

10

Next morning, I ran to the mirror in our hallway and pulled down the neck of my nightgown. I pushed up my sleeves, lifted my hem, and checked. No chicken pox. No spots. Not even a tiny rash. I felt my forehead. Rats. Cool as a cucumber.

I sat down at the table, trying my best to look green. "I don't feel so good."

"You look fine to me," Mom said, feeling my forehead. "Does she look sick to you, Larry?"

Pop slurped his cowpoke coffee. "Sick? No, I'm not sick."

"Ruthie," Mom said. "It's Ruthie. Does she look sick to you?"

"No. She looks fit as a fiddle."

"I'm *not* fit as a fiddle. See?" I stuck out my tongue.

They didn't look.

"My belly hurts." I pushed back my oatmeal and held my stomach. "I think I might throw up any second."

Mom opened the kitchen cabinet and pulled out her bottle of Dr. Jeever's Get Up and Go, which Violet and I called Dr. Jeever's Go Ahead and Die. It was our mothers' cure for everything that ailed us.

"Here you go. Take a nice big spoonful."

"Oh, Mom, that stuff is nasty. It tastes like puke."

"Now, Ruthie, do as you're told."

I closed my eyes. The slimy, sour green liquid filled my mouth and oozed down my throat. My whole body shook; my hands felt clammy. Sweat dripped down my neck.

Mom pushed my bowl of oatmeal in front of me.

"But I feel—"

"No buts. Eat."

I ate my oatmeal while Mom brushed and braided my hair, tying it with the same ugly brown ribbons.

That reminded me. "Mom, Pop, guess what? I get to sing the solo in our Christmas Tree Celebration."

Mom looked at her watch. "Better get goin'."

"Didn't you hear me? I get to be soloist. Fourth year in a row!"

"That's nice," they both said. But I could tell they didn't want to talk about it.

I tugged on my woolen wrap and tromped through the snow to our barn.

Daisy and her kittens were up in the hayloft, their new hiding spot. I petted Cinnamon and Nutmeg, their bellies round and warm, then dangled a piece of bacon in front of Daisy's nose.

She gulped it down and sniffed my fingers for more.

"No more. See?"

She rubbed against my legs and jumped into my lap, stretching her paws onto my shoulder. Her purry voice filled my ears.

"Oh, Daisy." I twirled my hair round and round. "What am I supposed to tell everyone at School District 42? Elden Larrs is probably making plans this very minute to humiliate me in front of everybody."

"Skip school? Are you serious?"

"Yes! We could camp right here in the depot. We could make a fire on those cinder blocks over there and cook our potatoes ourselves." I lifted my potato from my pocket. "What do you say?"

"I say you've gone berserk."

"Ah, come on, Vi. You don't want to be a stupid ol' donkey in the play, do you?"

"Well, no."

"Then stay here with me."

"Heavens to Betsy!" Violet said, smelling my breath. "Have you been drinking Ol' Man Rhemmer's whiskey?"

"Worse. Dr. Jeever's Go Ahead and Die!" I looked at the floor. "Come on, Vi. It'll be fun. Like camping out at Quartz Mountain, only we'll be right here in the depot."

Violet felt my forehead.

I blinked back tears.

40

"What's wrong, Ruthie?"

"Nothing."

"Ruthie, something's wrong. Now 'fess up." Violet grabbed my hands and looked into my eyes.

I hated when she did that. It was almost as if she looked into my very soul and I couldn't hide a thing. "Oh, Vi, something awful's happened."

"What?"

"I can't tell you."

"Can't *tell* me? Of course you can. When have you not been able to tell me something?"

"Now."

"Well, I've always told *you* everything, haven't I?"

Violet was right. I knew she was sweet on Miss Holman's nephew, Jim Holman, from Chicago. I knew he'd kissed her on Lovers' Lane while he was visiting last summer. I even knew she secretly wrote him love letters in pig Latin and signed them "oveLay ioletVay."

"Ruthie? Come on, you can tell me on our way to school."

"No, Vi." I plopped down on the cold wooden floor of the boxcar. "You go on."

"I'm *not* leaving without you." She sat beside me, yanking off her mitten with her teeth, and held out her pinky. "Friends till the cow jumps over the moon?"

Good old Vi. "And the dish runs away with the spoon." Then out it came, my deepest, darkest secret ever. And Violet cried right along with me.

11

"What's the big idea?"

I cringed in my seat. *Oh, why did I let Vi talk me into going to school?*

"I said, what's the big idea?"

"I'm sorry, Elden. Daphne didn't mean it. Honest. She was just trying to get Elizabeth's blanket. You know how she likes soft things."

"Ding-Dong Daffy chokes my sister half to death, makes her face turn blue, and all you have to say is *sorry?*"

I gasped. "Oh, Elden! Did Elizabeth's face really turn blue?" My hands shook. I felt faint. "Is—is she going to be all right?"

"How are we supposed to know? She's too little to talk. She can't tell us if she's dyin'."

"Shh." I looked over my shoulders. "Do you really think

she'll die?" My heart felt as if it was pumping right out of my chest.

"Heck if I know."

"I'm really sorry. Is there anything I can do?"

Elden eyed me up and down. "Well . . ." He hesitated, then lifted his eyebrows. "For starters, you could give me a kiss."

"A *kiss*?" The thought of kissing Elden made my toenails curl. How could he even *think* of kissing at a time like this? "Never."

"Then I'll tell everyone here what Ding-Dong Daffy did to sweet, innocent Elizabeth."

"Her name is Daphne, and you wouldn't dare."

"I wouldn't?" He grabbed R. W. McBee, who was walking by our desks. "Hey, R.W. Guess what happened when my mom and baby sister went to Tillman's Mer—"

"All right, all right," I said. "Where?"

"Around back. Lovers' Lane."

R.W. snickered. "Lovers' Lane? What are you two gonna do back there? Huh, huh, huh?"

"N-none of your business," I stammered. "Go sit down."

"But I didn't get to finish hearing what happened to Elden's mom and—"

"It was nothing," I said. "Nothing important. Now go sit down."

When R.W. was out of earshot, Elden leaned up close, his breath hot on my neck. "I thought you'd come to your senses."

I felt like slugging him right in the mouth. Maybe I could chip his other front tooth. Then he'd have a matched set.

"So how about today? After lunch?"

Today? I needed time to get out of this. "How about to-morrow?"

"Today."

"Tomorrow."

"Today. After lunch. Lovers' Lane."

My toenails were curling right out of my boots.

As usual, the dogs were fighting under our schoolhouse.

Every morning, Clyde Bushyhead's old, blind beagle, Stinky, followed him to school. And every morning, May-belle Smith's hound dog, Pot Licker, followed *her* to school.

Stinky and Pot Licker didn't get along very well, especially in the cold weather. They fought over which one was going to sit in the warm spot under the schoolhouse where the coal stove warmed down through the floorboards.

Some mornings they'd fight a good fifteen to twenty minutes, growling and yelping. Pot Licker, being lots bigger than Stinky, usually got the warm spot. Then we'd all have to listen to Stinky whine until Miss Holman broke down and let him inside.

Miss Holman always acted as if she didn't like Stinky. She said dogs didn't belong in the schoolhouse. But we knew she liked Stinky just as much as the rest of us.

"Did everyone read an article in *The Daily Oklahoman*?"

"Eww! Ewwww!"

"Yes, Howard?"

"I read about Shipwreck Kelly. People pay him to go around and sit on their flagpoles."

The class laughed.

"It's the latest rage," Howard went on, looking real serious. "Folks all over the nation are doin' it, but Shipwreck Kelly is the most famous. See, he sits on a small disk on top of a flagpole in front of new businesses, to help bring in customers. Last week, he was sittin' on a flagpole in front of a hotel in Dallas. While he was up there, the hotel elevator girl was hoisted up to give him a thermos of hot coffee. Just like that, they fell in love. After he came down, they got married!"

"What a story," Miss Holman said, smiling. "Anyone else?"

Elden raised his hand.

Miss Holman looked surprised. "And what did *you* read, Elden?"

"I read that drop-seat underwear are on sale for thirty-nine cents over in Lone Wolf."

Everyone cracked up.

Miss Holman gave Elden her evil-eye look, the one she must have learned in college for boys like Elden, where her eyes close halfway and her lips purse together. "Into the corner, young man!"

Elden clunked his bulky boots down the aisle, making

catcalls as he went by Maybelle's desk and enjoying the ruckus.

"Now, don't move an inch, or I'll get out my paddle." Miss Holman pointed his nose toward the corner.

I crossed my fingers and wished he'd move an inch. Then he'd be too sore to walk out back to Lovers' Lane. Things were looking up.

Under the schoolhouse, Stinky was really howling.

"Good gravy!" Miss Holman covered her ears. "Will somebody let that poor old dog in?"

Clyde ran to the door and whistled. A gust of cold air blew our papers as Stinky hobbled inside, sniffing his way from desk to desk, licking our fingers, then claiming his rightful place by the coal stove.

"I do declare," Miss Holman said, fanning the air. "That dog is full of wind. What do you feed him, Clyde?"

Clyde shrugged. "Well, my ma cleaned out the icebox yesterday. I think she gave him some leftover boiled cabbage and cauliflower."

Miss Holman pinched her nose and shooed Stinky to the far end of the schoolhouse. "You stay here, boy. Stay."

But we all knew he'd make his way back to the coal stove in just a matter of minutes. Being half blind and totally stinky didn't keep him from being a good navigator.

"Now then, who else has read a newspaper article?"

I raised my hand.

"Ruth Ann?"

"I read about a new songwriter turned composer named

George Gershwin. He uses common, everyday things in his musical compositions, like tin pans, wooden spoons, even auto horns. His latest composition, *Rhapsody in Blue*, is a big hit on Broadway."

"I've heard about him," Miss Holman said. "Ruth Ann, if you keep singing like you do, maybe one day *you'll* be on Broadway in a George Gershwin musical."

Me? In one of George Gershwin's musicals? Singing? Dancing like a flapper with my socks rolled down? I couldn't think of anything else I'd rather do.

"Will you remember us when you get rich and famous?" Miss Holman teased.

My cheeks felt flush. Everyone turned to look at me.

Elden pulled his nose out of the corner and put his hand over his heart. "Will you remember me?"

I couldn't forget Elden if I tied a rock around him and threw him in the deepest ocean.

12

When Miss Holman announced lunch, my heart sank into my boots.

"Line up, everyone. Ruth Ann, you look pale. Are you feeling all right?"

I wanted to scream, "No! I'm feeling terrible! Save me!" But instead I said, "Yes, ma'am," and laid my head on my desk.

Elden poked me in the neck with his pencil. "Don't fake a bellyache."

Violet made her way through the line, then rushed over to me. "Ruthie, you're as white as snow. What's happened? Has Elden said something to you?"

I looked over both shoulders to make sure no one was listening. "He said if I didn't kiss him, he'd tell everyone what Daphne did to Elizabeth."

"He didn't!"

"He did!" My eyes filled with tears.

"So when do you have to kiss him?"

"Today. After lunch. On Lovers' Lane." I laid my head back on my desk.

"Lovers' Lane? Oh, Ruthie, that's downright horrid! There's bound to be a way out of this. He's the most disgusting boy in School District 42!"

I lifted my head. "Don't remind me."

Old half-blind Stinky hobbled around the room, sniffing the air. He stopped at my desk and licked my hand.

"Get down, Stinky." I was in no mood for a dog kiss.

He licked my other hand.

"Yuck! Stinky, quit kissing me. Go lie—" An idea popped into my mind, an idea so perfectly splendid, it made me sit up and smile. "I've got it!"

"What?"

"Stinky!"

"What about him?"

I held out my hand and let Stinky give it another dog kiss. "See? Stinky's the answer to my problem!"

"Oh my word! That's *brilliant*!" Violet laughed so hard, potato spewed all over my arm.

"What's so funny?" Elden sat down behind us. "Are you two tellin' jokes?"

I burst out laughing, and Violet laughed even harder.

"Did you hear the one about the giant who threw up?"

We stifled our laughs and managed to say no.

"It's all over town! Get it? *All over town?*"

I wrinkled my nose. "That's not funny."

Elden smiled his chipped-tooth smile. After a few bites of potato, he nodded toward the back of the schoolhouse. "Ready for dessert?"

Dessert? Oh, brother!

He placed his hand on my shoulder and puckered his lips like a fish. "You can't resist these babies, can you?"

If he only knew. "Um . . . Elden? Can you wear a blindfold?"

"A blindfold? Don't tell me you're playin' shy."

"Well, you know me." I batted my eyelashes, trying to cover my laugh with a fake cough. Violet caught on, and started fake coughing, too.

"Here," I said, digging my ugly brown ribbons from my pocket. "Go on out there and put these on."

"Why should I?"

I twirled my hair. "Don't tell me you've never kissed a girl with a blindfold on before."

He puffed out his chest. "Maybe I have. Maybe I haven't."

"If you *have*, then you know how exciting it can be."

Violet really coughed at that one.

"Oh? Yeah. You're right."

"Of course I'm right." I pushed his hand off my shoulder. "It'll be the most exciting kiss you've ever had."

"It better be." He buttoned his coat and breathed into my ear. "I've been dreaming about this kiss for a looooooooong time."

"Really?" My stomach curdled.

"Really." Then he ran out the door like a pig chasing slop.

Violet laughed out loud. "You think it'll work?"

"It better. Here, Stinky! Here, boy!"

Stinky came hobbling over, his tail wagging so hard his whole body wagged with it.

"You be a good boy and I'll give you my *whole* potato. But first, I've got a little job for you . . ."

13

Snow crunched under my boots as I made my way around the back of the schoolhouse and through the cedars that hid Lovers' Lane.

There stood Elden, his lips all puckered as if he'd just eaten a lemon, his arms outstretched.

"Can you see?" I shouted, hiding behind a cedar. Stinky wriggled in my arms, stinking up a storm and making my eyes water.

"Heck, no, I can't see nothin'. Where ya at, you shy thing you?"

I inspected his blindfold from a distance. To make sure he really couldn't see, I threw a snowball to his left.

He turned, flailing his arms. "Where ya at?"

I slowly stepped closer and closer. *Come on, Stinky. Don't let me down. You can do it.*

"Don't play shy with me," Elden said. "Put it here, baby cakes!"

Baby cakes? I positioned Stinky's lips right in front of Elden's, but Stinky wouldn't hold still.

"I'm waiting . . ."

"Just a minute," I said. "These things take time, you know." *Come on, boy. You can do it.* I pushed Stinky's mouth onto Elden's, and he gave Elden a great big, wet, slobbery kiss. Right on the lips.

"Oh, baby!" Elden tried to grab me. I stepped back, but not far enough, and his hand grabbed Stinky's tail. "Gotcha. You know these braids of yours drive me hog wild!"

Stinky didn't take kindly to having his tail pulled. He twisted and turned, letting out a gust of wind that smelled like boiled cabbage.

"P.U. What's that smell?" Elden let go of Stinky's tail.

"Smell? I don't smell anything." Stinky flopped out of my arms, landing with a yelp.

"What was that?" Elden yanked the ribbons from his eyes. "Stinky? What's *he* doing out here?"

I swallowed hard. "Um . . . he must have followed me. That's right, he followed me. You know how he is, always comin' and goin'. Funny that way, isn't he?"

Elden eyed me. "You know, that kiss was awful quick."

"A deal's a deal." I started back through the cedars toward the schoolhouse.

"Not so fast." He grabbed my arm. "You know what I think?"

My heart jumped clear out my ears. *He's figured it out. He's going to blab to everyone about what Daphne did. Me and my bright ideas.*

"I think that was the best kiss I ever got."

"What? I mean, you do?"

"Yup. Let's do this again tomorrow."

"Never in a million years!"

"Aw, come on. Didn't that kiss mean anything? You know you like kissin' me, or you wouldn't have done it."

"I had no choice, remember? You blackmailed me."

Elden hung his head. "You didn't like it? Not even a teeny-tiny, little bit?"

For a moment, I almost felt sorry for Elden. But then I came to my senses. "I'd rather kiss the south end of a north-bound mule!"

And I ran into the schoolhouse.

The empty boxcar echoed with laughter as I acted out the kissing scene between Elden and Stinky in front of Violet.

"He never caught on?" Violet laughed so hard, she cried.

"Nope. In fact, he said it was the best kiss he'd ever had!"

"It's probably the *only* kiss he's ever had."

Our laughs turned into snorts. We must have sounded like two little pigs. Finally we caught our breath.

"What did Miss Holman say when you asked if she made a mistake about you being the donkey?"

Violet sighed. "She said it was no mistake, that I'm the donkey and Clyde and Ruby are dancing snowflakes."

"Did you ask if there could be *three* snowflakes?"

"Yeah, but she said she needed a donkey."

"So are you going to do it?"

"I have no choice. It's either donkey or stage cleanup. And stage cleanup is even worse! Remember last year, when Clayton got sick and puked?"

I put my arm around her. "Well, I think you'll make a fine donkey."

"Really?"

"Really."

"No teasing?"

"No teasing."

Violet got down on all fours. "How's this look?"

"Like a donkey."

"Oh, good." She stood up again. "And this?" She hee-hawed in her best donkey voice, lifting her lips to show her gums.

"Let's just put it this way, Vi. There better not be a male donkey in the audience, or you'll have yourself a boyfriend!"

14

I had no more than put down my books and pulled out a stick of licorice from the candy jar when Mrs. Larrs waltzed into our mercantile. She sauntered up and down the aisles, looking at hair tonics, sewing needles, and laxatives. Baby Elizabeth wasn't with her. And I could tell she wasn't shopping; she was snooping.

"Hello, Mrs. Larrs," I said, twirling my hair. I wanted to ask her about Elizabeth, but the words stuck in my throat.

Mom came out of the storeroom with a crate of oranges. "Well, Mrs. Larrs. What a surprise!" I could tell by Mom's voice, she didn't know what to say any more than I did.

"Yes, I suppose." Mrs. Larrs picked up a bottle of Carter's Little Liver Pills and put it right back down.

"So . . ." Mom handed me the orange crate. "How's baby Elizabeth?"

Mrs. Larrs looked at Mom, then at me and Pop. "Doc Bailey said not to worry, that she's as well as can be expected. Won't hardly eat anything and cries all day."

"Oh, I'm so sorry," Mom said. But I knew as well as Mom and Pop that baby Elizabeth always cried a lot. She was just one of those babies—the kind nobody liked to sit behind in church because she screamed loud enough to wake the dead, and of course anybody who happened to fall asleep during the sermon.

"We're truly sorry for what happened . . ." Mom's voice trailed off. "I promise, it'll never happen again."

"You bet it won't." Mrs. Larrs didn't smile.

"Anything we can get for you today?" Pop asked. "Just got a new shipment of brown sugar, straight from Hawaii, and I know how you love to make those brown-sugar cookies of yours. Here, let me give you a sack."

"I'm not here to shop." Mrs. Larrs adjusted her hat. It had a large purple plume that flopped down in her eyes, over a fishnet that covered half her face. "I'm here to relay a message."

"A message?" Pop rubbed his chin. "What kind of message?" The veins on his forehead were beginning to show. He tapped his fingers on the counter like four tiny racehorses.

"Well—" Mrs. Larrs stopped and gave me a dirty look.

I quickly started unloading oranges.

"As I was about to say," Mrs. Larrs continued, brushing

specks of melted snow from her coat, "Mr. Larrs and I feel that, well, Daphne is——" She stopped and looked at me again. "Young lady, it isn't polite to eavesdrop."

Mom shooed me outside, closing the door. *I hate being a kid.*

I ran around to the side window. Climbing up on an old pickle barrel, I peeked inside.

Pop looked horrible. Veins were popping out all over his forehead. His nostrils flared. I couldn't see Mom, because her back was toward me, but I could tell by the way she was pacing, she didn't like what Mrs. Larrs was saying, either.

Pop raised his fist. His face looked meaner than a riled possum's. He said something, then grabbed Mrs. Larrs's arm and ushered her out the front door.

I jumped down from the pickle barrel and stuck my head around the corner.

". . . and don't you *ever* set foot in my store again!" Pop slammed the door in her face.

Mrs. Larrs stood there, hands on hips, looking madder than a wet hen. "Well, I never——"

Then Mom opened the door. "And those brown-sugar cookies of yours taste like *soap*!"

Slam!

I covered my mouth laughing, watching Mrs. Larrs crank her Tin Lizzy. *Serves her right, the ol' biddy. I hope it doesn't start—I hope it spits and sputters and sticks its tongue out at her.*

But it started right up and took her mean old self out of sight.

15

"... fifty-seven, fifty-eight, fifty-nine, sixty!"

As usual, Daphne was making Josephine's only hand touch every square of our quilt; jumping on the bed with her nightgown tucked inside the waistband of her underwear; and holding up her arm like the Statue of Liberty.

"For goodness sake, Daphne Sue. Why do you always have to do this?"

"Kitties. Soft? Soft kitties." She plopped down next to me, stretching her legs all the way down to the hot brick at the foot of our bed. Lately, her legs had gotten quite hairy, and I didn't like the feel of them next to mine.

"Daphne, maybe you should start shaving your legs. All the grown girls are doing it, you know." The image of Daphne with a razor in her hands popped into my mind. "On second thought, don't. They're not *that* hairy."

I rolled over and faced the window.

"Kiss!" She pushed Josephine in my face.

"Stop. I don't want to kiss her."

"Kiss!"

"No."

Daphne threw the quilt on the floor. "Kiss! Kiss! Kiss!" She rattled the bedsprings.

"What's going on in here?" Mom asked, opening our door.

"She wants me to kiss her dumb doll."

"Ruthie"—Mom sat on the edge of our bed—"it's just a simple kiss. If that's all it takes to make her happy, you can do that."

"No I can't." I wasn't about to give in. "Every night she makes me kiss her cheek, her other cheek, her forehead, her dumb doll. She stands up like the Statue of Liberty with her gown tucked in her underwear. She counts quilt squares! I'm tired of it, Mom. Can't I have my own bedroom?"

Mom smoothed my hair. There was no other bedroom to have, and we'd had this conversation many times before.

"Here, Daphne," Mom said. "Let *me* kiss Josephine tonight. There. Is that better?"

"Soft. Soft. Love."

"Now, both of you, sleep!"

———

When Daphne's breathing grew slow and steady, I slipped out of bed and tiptoed through the darkness into the hallway. I pressed my ear against the kitchen wall.

Spoons tinkled.

The grandfather clock ticked.

". . . the nerve of that woman," Mom said. "How dare she say that Daphne is a danger to our community! Who does she think she is?"

A fist pounded the table. Then Pop bellowed, "Can you believe she had the audacity to say we should send Daphne away or lock her in a cage, like some kind of animal?"

Send Daphne away? Lock her in a cage? I wrapped my arms around myself, shivering.

"Mrs. Larrs must have blabbed to everyone in Kiowa County about what happened yesterday," Mom said. "Every customer who came in was quiet as all get-out. No one whispered a word. Not even Miss Willowbright, and that ol' gal can talk the hind leg off a hound dog."

A chair scooted.

Cups clattered.

"Do you think we've made the right decision about Ruthie bird?"

My heart skipped a beat. *What* decision?

"I think so," Mom said.

"Then I'll tell her tomorrow morning at breakfast."

"Wait until Monday morning. That way she won't mope around all weekend."

Mope around all weekend? What were they talking about?

"I'll tell her plain and simple," Pop said. "I'll sit Ruthie down and say, 'Ruthie bird, your mom and I have decided you can't—"

I stepped a little closer, right onto the creaky floorboard. *Screak!*

"Shh," Mom said. "Did you hear that? Sounds like one of the girls is up. Go take a look."

I froze in my tracks.

A chair scooted.

Footsteps.

I held my breath.

The kitchen door opened, letting light flood the hallway as I pressed behind the door.

"No, I don't see anyone," Pop said. "Must have been the wind."

He closed the door, and I scrambled over the tattletale floorboard, jumping into bed not a moment too soon.

Mom rushed into our room, shining her lantern. "Look at them . . . sleeping like angels."

If they only knew.

16

Monday morning took forever to arrive, and when I walked into the kitchen, Pop acted rather odd. He fiddled with his fork and salted his eggs twice. He cleared his throat several times, and I noticed Mom nodding to him when she thought I wasn't looking. Then I heard a bump under the table, as if Pop had been kicked.

At that point, Pop blurted out, "Ruthie bird, your mother and I have decided you can't sing the solo in the Christmas Tree Celebration."

I dropped my fork, egg and all. "Wh-what?"

"You heard me." He slurped his cowpoke coffee.

"B-but why?"

Mom put her arm on my shoulder and told me what had happened with Daphne and baby Elizabeth.

I eyed them both. "I already knew that."

They looked up, surprised. "You did? How?"

"Elden," I lied. I couldn't very well say I'd been eavesdropping.

"I see," they both said at the same time. I could tell they were feeling very awkward, and so was I.

"But I sing the solo every year." Tears filled my eyes.

"This year is different," Pop said. Putting down his coffee cup, he took my hand. "Ruthie bird, we don't want you to get hurt."

My hands trembled. I felt sick. "Hurt how?"

"People can be cruel. They can say mean things. We're worried that if you sing, there might be some folks who'll cause a ruckus about it."

"Like Needle-nose Larrs?"

"Yes." Pop patted my hand.

"So what does she have against *me*? *I'm* not the one who almost smothered baby Elizabeth. Oh, I get it. She thinks I'm crazy like my sister, doesn't she?"

"Ruthie!" Mom looked aghast.

"Well? *Is* that what she thinks?"

"Who knows," Pop said. "But the important thing is, we want to protect you."

"Protect me? Protect me from *what*?"

"Rumors. Gossip. You know how folks talk."

I sure did. I was used to it. Growing up with Daphne for an older sister, I had heard tons of rumors. Rumors about her, about me, about Mom and Pop, about how Daphne came to be the way she was.

"But we've lived with rumors! Why does this time have to be different from any other?"

"Because this time Daphne almost killed a baby."

I swallowed hard.

"It's for your own good, honey."

"Ruthie bird, there's always next year."

But who knew what next year would bring? Maybe next year, Daphne would find another way to humiliate our family. With Daphne for a sister, I had no idea what would happen. And I hated her for that.

17

"Well?"

"Well, what?"

"You're dragging your feet like flat tires!" Violet hopped out of the depot. "I thought you'd *never* get here!"

Brushing off the snow, I sat down on the steps.

"Ruthie, what are you doing?"

"Nothing."

Violet put her hands on her hips. "Let's go—we'll be late for school."

"Go on, then."

Violet looked into my eyes. "Ruthie, what's wrong?"

"Why do you always have to do that?"

"Do what?"

"Stare right through me?"

"Because I know you, Ruth Ann Tillman. Now out with it. You're as cranky as a dog full of fleas."

"Am not."

"Are too."

"Not."

"Too."

"Oh, Vi." And out it came. "Pop said I can't sing the solo in the Christmas Tree Celebration, and I have to tell Miss Holman to choose someone else, and Mrs. Larrs said Daphne should be locked up in a cage, and—"

"Whoa. Wait a minute. Now tell me what happened nice and slow, from the beginning."

I told her everything—everything, all the way down to Mrs. Larrs's brown-sugar cookies tasting like soap.

Violet covered her grin. "Good, maybe now she won't bring those nasty cookies to our church suppers anymore. You know I've always thought they tasted just like—"

"Vi?" I twirled my hair. "Do you think I'm like my sister?"

"Well, in some ways, yes."

"What ways?"

"Um, you both look like your mom. But you have your pop's nose. And you're both funny and you both like cheese sandwiches with mustard and—"

"No, I mean am I *like* my sister?"

"Heavens, no! What made you ask?"

"I was just wondering. You know how folks like to spread rumors and all."

"Yes, but folks ought to know by now that you and your sister are two different people. Besides, Daphne doesn't

in to do what she does. She may not have much sense,
but that doesn't make her a baby killer."

Baby killer. Hearing those words made me want to run
and hide. "Vi, just because Daphne isn't a baby killer,
doesn't mean she *can't* be. Don't you see? If Elizabeth hadn't
let out one of her bloodcurdling screams the other day, she
might have ended up just like Boots."

"Don't be silly."

"I'm *not* being silly. You don't understand. You don't
know what it's like. *Your* sister's married to a banker in
Florida and has palm trees in her front yard!"

Violet started to say something, then stopped and hung
her head.

"I'm sorry, Vi." I could tell she had news about LeNora.
She *always* had news about LeNora. "Go ahead. Tell me."

"No, I shouldn't."

"It's all right. Go ahead."

"Well, we got a Christmas card from LeNora. She's built
a new studio onto her home. That way she can keep up with
her photography. She sent us a photo of little Cecil; he's a
doll! I wanted to bring it to show you, but Mom wouldn't
let me. And guess what?" She got that proud look on her
face, the one she always got when she was talking about her
sister.

"What?"

"She's expecting again! You'll never believe what she's
going to name it if it's a girl." Violet beamed. "Violet—
Violet Abigail—just like me! Isn't that the berries?"

I kicked a clod of snow. "I hate this snow. It's so . . . so white and cold and wet. We don't need this stuff. What's it good for, anyway?"

Violet eyed me. "Snow is supposed to be white and cold and wet. Just look at Quartz Mountain all powdered in snow. It looks pretty as a postcard. Say, do you think I should send a postcard to Jim Holman in Chicago? I could write in pig Latin, 'erryMay istmasChray, oveLay, ioletVay.' "

I shook my head.

"Why not?"

I couldn't tell her the real reason, that I was a miserable wreck and wanted her to be miserable right along with me. So I lied. "Because—because he's ugly."

"Ugly? He's not, either."

"Then what's that big mole on his chin?"

"Mole?"

"Right under his lip. Big as a dime."

"Big as a dime? You mean that little tiny freckle?"

"It's big as a quarter, and you know it."

"It's a *freckle*," Violet said, crossing her arms.

"Your neck is getting all red and blotchy."

"It is not."

"Is, too." I couldn't help but smile.

"You know what I think? You're jealous, Ruth Ann Tillman. Downright jealous."

"Now, why would I be jealous of an ugly boy with a mole the size of a silver dollar?"

"You're not jealous of him."

"Oh yeah, Miss Know-It-All? Then who am I jealous of?"

"My sister!"

Why did Violet always have to be right?

18

"Hurry, everyone!" Miss Holman flapped around the schoolhouse like a barnyard chicken on a windy day. "Put your potatoes in the tin! Hang up your coats and wraps! The ladies from the Quartz Mountain Sewing Circle should be here any minute!"

I dropped my potato into the five-gallon coffee tin.

"So, are you going to tell Miss Holman?" Violet dropped her potato on top of mine.

"No."

"She needs to know so she can find someone else to sing the solo."

"No, she doesn't."

"I thought you said you weren't allowed—"

"Shh." I covered her mouth. "I'm going to change Mom and Pop's mind. So hush up!"

A burst of cold air rushed into the schoolhouse as three

gray-headed ladies, all bundled in woolen wraps, scarves, and gloves, tromped inside, stomping snow from their boots.

"I'm *so* glad you made it!" Miss Holman looked relieved.

Then the door opened again, and in shuffled an old man with a cane. He sat down by the stove and started warming his hands.

"My husband, Herman, nearly turned around and drove back home," one lady said. "But when he thought of these youngsters with no costumes for their play, he decided to give it another try."

"We certainly appreciate it, don't we children?"

Everyone clapped. Then Miss Holman said, "Line up! Angels over there! Sheep and camel right here! Santa! Where's Santa?"

Marvin Tallchief answered with a "Ho, ho, ho!"

The three gray-headed ladies got down to business. "Arms up. Shoulders back," they barked.

Measuring tapes flew from the ladies' fingers, straight pins appeared out of their mouths, scissors snapped like alligators. "Looks like three yards of red. No, make that three and a half, and two yards of white. Next!"

Miss Holman nudged me forward. "Here's our soloist."

Violet cleared her throat.

"Ruth Ann will be wearing the blue velvet with silver ribbons in her hair," Miss Holman said.

Violet elbowed me. "Tell Miss Holman what your parents said."

I could have clobbered her.

"What did they say?" Miss Holman asked.

My heart jumped into my throat. "Um." I crossed my fingers behind my back. "Well . . . they said they can't wait for the Celebration . . . and they're right proud of me singing the solo."

"Oh, good," Miss Holman said.

Violet gave me a dirty look.

I gave her one right back.

I eyed the blue velvet and ran my finger along its soft nap, softer than a horse's nose. The silver ribbon was so shiny and beautiful, I couldn't resist holding up the spool to my brown braid just to see how it gleamed.

"Oh, won't that look dandy?" said one of the ladies.

I swallowed hard, knowing I should tell the truth. But I held my arms out, shoulders high, and let the ladies measure me, feeling like a cooked goose.

19

After Herman and the Quartz Mountain Sewing Circle left, Miss Holman plopped down in her chair and gave us an indoor recess. Most of us gathered in groups, doing puzzles or scraping pictures in the frost on the windowpanes. Some scraped their initials. Others scraped snowmen. But the pictures would have looked much prettier without the thick steel netting on the outside of the windowpanes.

I was sitting at my desk, still fuming over Violet and her big mouth, when Maybelle, Ruby, and Howard walked by, snickering.

I watched them look and snicker. Snicker and look. Then Ruby spoke up: "Is it really true?"

"Is what really true?"

"That Daphne tried to kill Elden's sister the other day?"

"No, it's a lie! Don't you believe it! My sister would never do a thing like that!" My insides quivered and spun around.

"It is *too* the truth, and you know it." Maybelle smiled. "Howard's mother told Ruby's mother, and Ruby's mother told *my* mother—so it's *got* to be true."

I eyed Howard Sulkey, with his skinny little arms and his constant stupid questions. "Then Howard's mom doesn't know what she's talking about."

"Are you callin' my ma a liar?" He made a fist.

Howard's fist was frail as peanut brittle and wouldn't scare a cricket. "Yes," I said, twirling my hair. "She's a big fat liar."

"Why, I oughta—"

"Oughta *what*?" Elden stepped between us.

"I oughta punch Ruthie right in the mouth. She said my ma is a big fat liar."

Just what I needed. Elden. At a time like this.

Elden pushed little Howard away from my desk. "Get. Now, leave Ruthie alone. All of you!"

Maybelle pouted, looking hurt that Elden was sticking up for me. She put her arm on Elden's knee and tried to act buddy-buddy. "Well, *my* mom said that *Howard*'s mom said that *your* mom said Daphne tried to smother baby Elizabeth."

"My ma is always goin' around exaggerating. You know that."

"Well, we heard—"

"Then you heard wrong," Elden said. "My sister got tangled up in her blanket. That's all." And he shooed them away like flies on a summer day.

I eyed Elden. Was this the same Elden who made my toenails curl? The most disgusting boy in School District 42?

He sat down behind me. "You know that songwriter-turned-composer you read about in the newspaper?"

"George Gershwin?"

"Yeah. Well, um, I like him, too."

"You do?" I turned around, facing him. "Is this a joke or something?"

"Nope. I really like him. Did you know his last name used to be Gershvin with a *v*? He changed it to Gershwin because everyone kept pronouncing it wrong."

"Where's his family from?"

"Russia."

I braced myself, knowing any second he would pull a joke or say something horrid.

"You know *Rhapsody in Blue*?"

All right, here comes the joke. I nodded.

"My mom bought us a Victrola for Christmas, and we got Gershwin's new record with that song on it."

My heart leapt out of my chest. "You don't mean *Rhapsody in Blue*?"

"Uh-huh."

"And a *real* Victrola that plays music when you crank it, like old Miss Willowbright's?"

"Uh-huh."

"Really? No joke? You're not lying?"

"Cross my heart." He squirmed in his seat, then looked

up at the ceiling. "So, um, would you like to come over and, um, hear it sometime, maybe?"

"Would I?" My heart was still leaping. "But what about your mother? She wouldn't want me over there."

"Who says she has to know?"

"How could we keep it from her?"

"She takes a nap with Elizabeth at four o'clock every day, like clockwork. Come over sometime. She'll never know the difference."

20

"Well?" Mom asked, passing the butter beans around the table. "Did you tell Miss Holman you can't sing the solo in the Christmas Tree Celebration?"

"Not exactly."

"Either you did, or you didn't. Now, which is it?" Her hair was falling out of its bun, and I could tell she'd had a rough day.

I hung my head. "Please let me sing. I'll do anything. I'll scrub floors. I'll wash dishes. I'll pull weeds for the rest of my life!"

I turned to Pop. "Pop? Please? I'll sweep the mercantile every day after school, and I won't complain a bit."

Pop slurped his cowpoke coffee, looking just as down-trodden as Mom. "Sorry, Ruthie bird. The answer's still no. Pass the salt and pepper, please."

"But—"

"No buts. You can't sing, and that's our final decision."

I slumped in my chair.

"Beans. Beans. More."

Mom dished another serving of butter beans into Daphne's bowl. "I swear, this girl eats like a horse!"

Pop smiled. "She's a growin' girl, aren't you, Daphne?"

We ate our supper in silence.

As Mom was serving apple pie, Pop started talking about the new Charlie Chaplin movie playing at the Kiowa Theater over in Hobart. "Say, I read in *The Daily Oklahoman*, Charlie Chaplin makes over a million dollars a year." Pop cut off a triangle of his apple pie. "Ruthie bird, what would you do with a million dollars?"

That was easy. "I'd move to Hollywood, California, and become a famous jazz singer. I'd wear short dresses like the flappers wear, with strings and beads and my socks rolled down."

A horrified look spread across Mom's face. "You wouldn't!"

"I would."

Mom covered her ears. "Next thing you'll want to bob your hair."

"Oh, can't I, please? Miss Holman has *her* hair bobbed."

"And her mother should have a good talk with her. Decent girls don't go around cutting their hair. It's not right."

"It's all the rage in Hollywood."

"Hollywood, Follywood," Mom said, wiping Daphne's hands. "If everyone in Hollywood jumped off a cliff, would you jump, too?"

"No."

"Then there will be no hair bobbing in this house."

"Mom, there's a big difference between bobbing your hair and jumping off a cliff."

"Not as far as I'm concerned."

"Well, someday I'm going to bob my hair," I insisted. "And when I get rich and famous, I'm going to wear Flamingo Pink lipstick, just like Bessie Smith."

"Bessie Smith? Who in the world is that?"

I rolled my eyes. Sometimes Mom didn't know anything. "She's Empress of the Blues. Everybody knows that. 'Down Hearted Blues' has already sold over two million records!"

"And how do you know this empress wears Flamingo Pink lipstick?"

"Well, I'm not exactly sure. But I figure anybody as famous as she is *must* wear Flamingo Pink because it's the prettiest color there is."

"Lipstick, hair bobs, socks rolled down—I don't know what to do with you, Ruth Ann Tillman."

"You can let me sing in the Christmas Tree Celebration!"

"Nice try, Ruthie. But the answer's still no."

21

"So?"

"So what?"

"So why didn't you tell Miss Holman the truth yester-day?"

"Vi, don't worry about it." I threw a snowball at the de-pot before we headed to school along the tracks.

"But don't you think you should tell her?"

"I'll tell her. I just need some time, that's all." I turned and threw another snowball. "Vi, if I don't sing that solo, I'll just die."

"I know how you feel. That's how I felt when I didn't get to be a dancing snowflake. But you know what? I kind of like being the donkey. At least I get to say hee-haw. Danc-ing snowflakes don't say anything."

"But, Vi, don't you see? This could be the beginning of

my singing career. What if a talent scout is in the audience?"

"A talent scout?" Violet laughed. "Really, Ruthie. What would a talent scout be doing in a little town like this on Christmas Eve?"

Violet had a good point. But I didn't like her laughing at me. Especially with our last argument still hanging in the air. "Well, he could have heard about me. He could have come to hear me sing. He could have, you know."

Violet laughed even louder. "Oh, I'm sorry, Ruthie. I don't mean to laugh, but you're such a dreamer!"

"A dreamer?" I crossed my arms. "And what's wrong with being a dreamer? George Gershwin is a dreamer, and look at him—he makes music with pots and pans. Bessie Smith is a dreamer, and look at her— she's Empress of the Blues. I can be a dreamer if I want."

"Come on, we'll be late for school."

"Not so fast," I said, looking Violet in the eyes. "You act like being a dreamer is a bad thing."

"Well, sometimes it is."

"Why?"

"Because dreams don't always come true."

"So you're saying that no talent scout would ever be interested in me? Is that what you're saying?"

"No. I'm saying a talent scout wouldn't come here, to

Babbs Switch, Oklahoma, on Christmas Eve. Now hurry up, or I'm walking without you."

"Go on, then."

"Suit yourself."

But at the moment nothing suited me, especially not Miss Know-It-All.

22

After we looked up our spelling words, which took a long time since Elden hogged the dictionary looking for *booger* and *fart*, I mustered up the nerve to approach Miss Holman. I walked slowly to her desk, feeling everyone's eyes on the back of my head. "Um, Miss Holman? I, uh, need to talk to you."

Miss Holman took off her glasses, rubbing her eyes. "What is it, Ruth Ann?"

"Well, I . . . You see, my pop . . . I can't sing the solo in this year's Christmas Tree Celebration."

"Oh, Ruth Ann, I'm so sorry. Why not?"

"Mom and Pop said I can't."

"Is it because of Mrs. Larrs?"

Tears filled my eyes. "You know about what happened?"

Miss Holman nodded.

Tears ran down my cheeks.

Miss Holman patted my back and offered me her handkerchief. "Well, Ruth Ann, I'm glad you had the courage to tell me. I know how important this is to you. But there will be other solos. Maybe you can be soloist in our Easter Drama."

"Maybe." But right now, no other solo mattered.

"I saw you go up to Miss Holman's desk this morning." As usual, Violet sat next to me at the corner of the stage. "You did the right thing by telling her the truth." She put down her potato and looked into my eyes. "Ruthie, I'm really sorry you can't sing the solo."

"Me, too." I took a bite of potato.

Violet looked at the floor. "Well, um . . . did you notice Miss Holman called me to her desk after arithmetic?"

I nodded. "Did she make a mistake about you being the donkey?"

"Not exactly."

"What was it, then?"

"She asked me if I would sing the solo."

My heart jumped out onto my plate. "You turned her down, didn't you?"

"No."

"No? You mean you said *yes*? I can't believe this!" Every muscle in my body tensed. "Why are you doing this?"

"Miss Holman asked me to. She said if I didn't, she'd ask Maybelle, and we both know Maybelle can't carry a tune

85

in a bucket. She can't even *hum*. So I really had no choice."

I twirled my hair around and around, getting madder by the twirl.

"Come on, Ruthie. You know I wouldn't hurt you for the world."

"Then why are you singing my solo?"

"I already told you. And quit saying it's your solo. It's mine!"

"Fine."

"Fine."

"Who's going to play the donkey?"

"I am."

"You're going to sing *and* be the donkey?"

"Is there any rule I can't?"

I nodded, trying to understand. But I didn't. And I took it all out on Violet.

"Vi, if you sing my solo, I'll never forgive you. You— You *traitor*."

"Traitor?" Violet pretended to laugh. "You're the one who's a traitor."

"Me?"

"Yes, you! You know you can't sing that solo. But I can. You should be happy for me. But noooo, instead you raise a ruckus."

"Do not."

"Do too."

"Not."

"Too."

I finished my potato, then marched off to the bucket of water to scrub my fork and plate.

Violet plopped her plate in the water as I handed her the scrubber. "Let's not quarrel, Ruthie." She held out her pinky.

I folded it back down. "I don't lock pinkies with traitors. And one more thing. My name is Ruth Ann. Only my *friends* call me Ruthie."

"Then you just call me Violet because only *my* friends call me Vi."

23

I walked home real slow, listening to the snow crunch under my boots.

Violet ran on ahead of me, laughing and talking to Maybelle as if they were the best of pals. I knew she was chumming with Maybelle just to irritate me. It was working.

I stopped to watch Ol' Man Rhemmer's cows. They were all hunkered down next to their huge haystack, sheltered from the wind. One cow had dug a hole in the side of the hay, and lay there chewing her cud, all warm and cozy.

A couple of weeks ago, Mom had brought Daphne to school right about the time school let out. She told Daphne to walk home with me, while she and two other mothers helped Miss Holman fill goodie bags with candy and nuts for our celebration.

Daphne had made me stop at Ol' Man Rhemmer's

haystack, so she could dig her hands into the hay. "Warm," she had said. "Warm."

At the depot, I grabbed the white flag that people used to hail the engineer, and waved it back and forth, imagining . . .

Where ya headed, Miss?
Oh, anywhere. How about Tokyo? Or New Orleans?
  Or England, to meet the queen?

I pretended to step inside and take a seat. I felt the lurch of the train, heard the clickety-clacks of the wheels on the tracks, and watched Babbs Switch grow smaller and smaller until it was a speck on the horizon.

My fingers and toes were freezing, so I decided to go into the depot and warm up. I slid open the door.

"Boo!"

I jumped back, falling into a snowdrift.

"Elden Larrs! What in blue blazes are *you* doing here?"

"Me? Umm, I just stopped by to warm up."

"That's a lie. You live in the complete opposite direction." I climbed out of the snowdrift.

"Don't go."

"Why?"

" 'Cause I wanna talk."

"About what?"

"I don't know. Anything, really." He stood in the doorway, rubbing his hands together. "Come on in before you freeze."

Inside, I kept my eye on him. "Is this some kind of joke?"

"It ain't no joke. I just thought you might wanna talk." He paced the floor, his breath fogging the air. "So do ya think maybe you'll come over to hear our new Victrola? If we crank it good and hard, it'll play a long time."

I didn't answer, and my hand was still on the door handle.

"We got us another record, too, ya know. The fella who sold us the Victrola said it came with only one free record, but my mom talked him into two."

He had my curiosity up. "What other one did you get?"

"Bessie Smith, Empress of—"

"—the Blues!"

We stood there, looking at each other, smiling.

Then I had to know: "Have you heard her song 'Down Hearted Blues'?"

His eyes lit up. "It's sold nearly two million copies. Now *there*'s somebody who's rich and famous."

"Does her record have a picture on it?"

"Yep. And she's not white, either. Her skin's dark as molasses."

I imagined a lovely dark woman with pure black hair. "Does she have on Flamingo Pink lipstick?"

"Flamingo what?"

"Flamingo Pink lipstick!"

He shrugged his shoulders. "Heck if I know."

"When I get rich and famous, I'm going to wear Flamingo Pink everywhere I go, even when they feature me on the cover of *The Saturday Evening Post*."

"Well, um, if you want, you can come over and see what color lipstick she's wearin'."

I smiled, then felt a little embarrassed, talking to Elden about lipstick.

"You know all the stuff I said 'bout you not ever going to be rich and famous?"

I nodded.

"And that you can't sing worth a lick?"

I nodded.

"Well"—he looked up at the ceiling—"it's not true."

I looked up to see what he was looking at. Nothing.

"You really are a dandy singer," he continued, now looking down at the floor. "I ain't lyin'."

I wished with all my heart that Vi was standing beside me to witness Elden's apology. *She'll never believe this in a hundred blizzards!* Then I remembered she was a big fat traitor.

"And you know when I said you had a long, skinny neck and freckles and a crossed eye?"

I nodded.

"I didn't mean that, either."

"You didn't?"

"Maybe the crossed-eye part, but not the rest."

"Elden Larrs! I don't either have a crossed eye, and you know it."

"Do too."

"Do not."

"Too."

"Not."

"Elden Larrs, you're impossible. You're deplorable. You're the most dis—"

And he kissed me right on the lips.

24

The door creaked. The smell of hay filled my nose as I stepped inside the barn to check on Daisy's kittens.

"There you are!" Mom said, scaring the daylights out of me. She was all hunched over, mucking out Molly's stall, and didn't even look up. "I was beginning to worry. What took you so long?"

"Oh, nothing. I, um, just stopped by the depot to warm up."

"Was Violet with you?"

"Vi? Uh, no."

Mom stood up, wiping straw from her hair. "I swear, Molly does nothing but eat and poop!"

"Mom? Do my lips look okay? I mean, they're still there, aren't they?"

Mom put down her rake and looked at me kind of funny.

"What do you mean, 'They're still there, aren't they?' Of course they are. Is it *that* cold outside?"

I fingered my lips. Mom was right. They were still there. But I had a sneaky suspicion they'd fall off any minute after coming into contact with Elden Larrs. "Mom? Do I have a crossed eye?"

"A crossed *eye?*" Mom came out of the stall. "Who told you that?"

"Nobody." I flipped the handle back and forth on Molly's feed bucket. "Are you sure my eye's not crossed?"

"Sure I'm sure. Now, why are you asking all these silly questions?"

I pulled my button in and out of its buttonhole. "No reason, really."

Mom's eyebrows squeezed together. "Did you tell Miss Holman that you can't sing the solo?"

"Yes." My eyes filled with tears.

"Well? What did she say?"

"She asked me if it was because of Mrs. Larrs."

"So the whole town knows what Daphne did to Elizabeth?" Mom asked. But it wasn't really a question.

I nodded.

Mom wrapped her arms around me and burst into tears. "I'm at my wit's end, Ruthie. I don't know how to help Daphne."

I wanted to console her, to convince her Daphne was going to be all right. But lately, nothing was all right, everything was all wrong, and I didn't know how to change that.

Mom sniffled. "I've had so many dreams for you two. So *many* dreams. But for Daphne, they'll never come true."

And I realized right then, Mom needed Daphne to grow up and get married and live in a house with palm trees in her front yard just as much as I did.

25

Ping. Ting. Ping ting.

I lay in bed, listening to ice hit our windowpane. The air was so cold around the window that even with the curtains shut, I could still feel a draft.

In the bedroom darkness, I studied Daphne. If I didn't know her any better, I'd think she was just like everyone else's big sister—talking about boys, laughing at jokes, explaining all the fuss about s-e-x. But Daphne was like no one's big sister that I had ever known.

She loved "Jack and the Beanstalk," and no matter how many times we read it to her, each time was like the first.

She always hid in the same spot when it came time for Saturday night baths: behind the floor-length curtains in the parlor, where her feet would be sticking out.

Mom made her wear a bra, but she didn't like it. She'd yank it off, saying, "Bad bra! Bad bra!"

To see her, though, sound asleep next to me, no one would ever know.

Mom and Pop's low voices mingled with the chimes from our grandfather clock, but I didn't dare get up for more eavesdropping. I didn't need to feel any worse than I already did.

I rolled over on my belly, my back, my side. I couldn't sleep, thinking about the hurt look on Vi's face when I folded down her pinky.

Dear God,

I feel plumb awful about folding down Vi's pinky and telling her Miss Holman's nephew is ugly when he's really not that bad.

I know if things were turned around, and Miss Holman asked me to sing the solo in Violet's place, I'd have said yes, too.

Isn't there anything you can do? How about an old-fashioned miracle? It doesn't have to be fancy, like when you parted the Red Sea or spoke out of a burning bush in the Bible. But I guess you don't need me telling you how to run your business. What do I know? I'm just a kid. Amen.

Um, one more thing. Just between you and me and one or two of your angels, I'm kinda-sorta all mixed up

*about Elden Larrs and how he kept his promise and
didn't blab about Daphne when he had the perfect
chance. And how he likes Bessie Smith, Empress of the
Blues. And how when he kissed me in the depot today,
my spine tingled like a hedgehog and I can't seem to
think about anything else. Do you think I'm coming
down with something awful?*

26

The next day, Wednesday, we had our first practice. I hung around a while after school, pretending to look for something in my desk. I never did find what I was looking for, but I did get to hear everyone sing "O Christmas Tree."

Poor Maybelle. Miss Holman had to keep moving her farther and farther away from the rest of the group because she was making everyone else sing off key.

Friday, I stood in the back, taking my own sweet time putting on my wrap and mittens and scarf, listening as everyone went over their lines. They were doing pretty well, too, except for little Howard Sulkey. He kept foretting his lines, and finally Miss Holman taped them this shirt.

It's not fair. I trudged home alone. I stopped to wa Ol' Man Rhemmer's cows, but they weren't standing thei haystack. Instead, they were out in the open with i wind whipping around them. *Dumb cows. Dumb Christmas Tree Celebration. Dumb, dumb, dumb.*

On Saturday, I secretly harbored a hope that we'd go to Fix-Up Day at the schoolhouse. I fancied Pop bringing his paintbrushes and turpentine. Mom bringing her apricot bread with almond slices or a pot of her baked beans simmered in onions and molasses. Daphne and I stringing cranberries and laughing and sipping hot chocolate.

Instead, I watched our grandfather clock announce nine o'clock, ten o'clock, eleven.

I thumbed through the pages of our latest *Saturday Evening Post*. On the cover was an illustration by my favorite artist, Norman Rockwell. Inside were several models with waists as tiny as teakettles and their hair up in French twists.

By twelve, I knew everybody would be in full swing at the schoolhouse. They'd probably be painting and laughing at jokes and blackening the coal stove, maybe even uncovering all the good-smelling dishes the mothers had brought for lunch.

By one o'clock, my stomach was growling, imagining all the food—Mrs. McBee's sliced apples with melted caramels, Mrs. Rader's fried chicken dipped in cornflakes and buttermilk, Mr. Sulkey's hot crumbly cornbread that melted in my mouth, and Mr. Tallchief's red-hot chili, which everyone said was hotter than "you-know-where."

"Lucy!" Mom called, poking her head out the kitchen door. "Birdie? Go get Pop!"

I put down the magazine and walked through the store-room, which separated our house from the mercantile. "Pop?" I opened the red-checked curtain. "Mom says it's time to eat."

It seemed strange to see our mercantile so empty, even emptier than it had been right after the trouble with baby Elizabeth. Usually Saturdays were our busiest days. Folks were always running in for gasoline or this and that.

"I guess everyone must be at Fix-Up Day at the school-house," Pop said.

"Oh, Pop, can't we go, too?"

"No, Ruthie bird."

We dragged ourselves to the kitchen, where Mom and Daphne already sat at the table, eating leftover tomato soup and crackers.

"Hot. Hot soup."

"That's right, Daphne," Mom said. "Hot. Be careful."

Pop poured a cup of cowpoke coffee. I watched him crack an egg, throw the shell and all into the pot, give it a stiff stir, then sit down at the table.

If I hadn't been so miserable, I'd have poked fun at him, but I didn't say a word.

"Soft. Soft." Daphne stood on her chair, rubbing a slice of bread across her cheek. "Soft?"

I crumbled crackers in my soup, wishing with all my might that Violet would appear at our door, begging to please come to Fix-Up Day.

By three o'clock, I was pacing the floors. Why hadn't

27

den
ber

wc

y
g

s

Violet hooked her arm into mine. "Pretty, isn't it?"

I stood there, breathless, taking in the sight. "It's grand. Pure-dee-grand!"

Our one-room schoolhouse stood before me, transformed—the walls were white as snow, the coal stove was so shiny I could see my reflection, and draped around the windows were spruce trimmings and strings of shiny cranberries and red ribbon bows big as basketballs. It was truly a sight to behold.

"I missed you Saturday."

"You did?" I was glad.

"That Maybelle drives me nuts."

I was even more glad.

"All she does is talk about Elden. Elden this and Elden that. Can you imagine anyone in their right mind being sweet on *Elden*?"

I twirled my hair around and around.

"Oh, Ruthie, I'm sorry for our fight."

"I'm sorry, too."

"I wish you were the one singing this solo. I'm as nervous as a cat on a clothesline."

"You'll do fine, Vi." It felt good to call her Vi again. "Just pretend you're singing to an empty room."

"But that's just it—it won't be empty. There will be folks from Lone Wolf and Roosevelt and Hobart, and I just know I'll mess up."

"I'll be rooting for you."

"Really?"

"Really."

"You're not mad at me anymore?"

"No. It was all my fault, anyway."

Violet grabbed my hands. "Will you come to the Celebration?"

I lifted my shoulders. "Mom and Pop are pretty set on us not going."

"Can't you change their minds? You've got two more days to do it."

"I'll try, Vi. But don't count on it."

28

The next day, I tapped lightly on Elden's front door, looking over my shoulder to see if anyone was watching.

My Montgomery Ward wristwatch said four-fifteen on the dot.

"Well, look what the cat drug up!" Elden said, smiling. "I had a hunch you'd come over today."

"You did?"

"Yup. Come on in. Just got back from practice. Mom and Elizabeth are sound asleep."

I stepped inside, taking off my wrap and mittens.

"Want some buttermilk?"

"No, thanks."

"Aw, come on. How about some apple juice?"

"All right."

I followed him into the kitchen. It was pretty as a maga-zine—all decorated in blue and yellow, with wallpaper of blue morning glories, and yellow gingham curtains with little white puffballs hanging on the hems.

"My, your house is pretty!"

"Yeah, it'll do." Elden poured some apple juice. "Mom's always picking at me to clean up my messes and put things back where they belong. Is your mom that way?"

I nodded, but I had a feeling Elden's mom spent a lot more time cleaning and decorating than my mom.

"Well, here's our Victrola." Elden led me into the front parlor, which was even prettier than the kitchen, with a dark green sofa and two matching chairs, a delicate china vase shaped like a woman's head, a rock fireplace, and a Christmas tree so tall, its star touched the ceiling.

The walls were painted a soft mint green and topped with pink stenciled roses. "Did your mom do all this stenciling?"

"Yeah. She can't leave nothin' alone. Always has to make things look like a bunch of girls live here. Me and Dad don't like it much. You like it?"

"It's a *dream*."

Elden got up close to my ear. "I think you're a dream."

He closed the parlor door, cranked the Victrola, and just like that, *Rhapsody in Blue* began to fill the room.

I listened, spellbound.

"You like it?"

"Like it? I *love* it." I'd never heard anything more inspiring, more uplifting, more take-me-away.

When the music ended, I sat down on the sofa. "That

was magical!" Then I remembered the Flamingo Pink lipstick. "Where's your Bessie Smith record?"

Elden looked inside the wooden cabinet that held the Victrola. "Um, here it is." He put the record on and gave the Victrola a crank.

There, on the front cover, smiled Bessie Smith, Empress of the Blues, with jet-black eyes and skin as dark as chocolate.

Elden sat next to me on the sofa, looking at the album cover. He put his arm on the back of the sofa, just above my shoulders.

"Oh, fiddlesticks. I can't tell if she's wearing Flamingo Pink."

"Your lips are so pretty, they don't need lipstick."

"They don't?"

"Nope."

I twirled my hair around and around.

"So, are ya comin' to the Celebration tomorrow night?" He scooted closer.

"Probably not." I scooted away.

"Why?" He scooted closer. His arm dropped down on my shoulder. I kind of liked it being there.

"Pop's worried about people talking and such." I bit my lip.

We sat there, listening to the music, with the fireplace popping and Elden's arm around me. It was so nice and cozy, I didn't want to move.

After a while, Elden put his finger on the tip of my nose.

"You're crazy-mad-in-love with me, Ruth Ann Tillman, and you know it."

"I do, too. I mean, I do not!" That same feeling tingled up and down my spine. I tried to scoot away, but there was no sofa left, and I landed on the floor.

Crash! The delicate china vase in the shape of a woman's head fell right along with me.

"Matthew Elden?" yelled a voice. "What did you break?"

Elden's face turned white. He put his finger on my lips. "Nothin'! I didn't break nothin'!"

"Then what was that racket?"

"Racket? What racket?" He started kicking pieces of the vase under the sofa.

"I heard something break—now, what was it?"

"Nothin'!"

"I know I heard some—" Mrs. Larrs opened the parlor door. "My beautiful vase! My grandmother's vase!" She picked up a piece of the woman's nose and one ear.

"It was me, Mrs. Larrs. I broke your vase. I'm sorry, I—"

"*You?* What are *you* doing in my house?"

"I invited her," Elden said, stepping between us. "I wanted her to hear our Victrola."

Mrs. Larrs picked up the other ear and the lips. "You're probably happy about this, aren't you?"

"No, ma'am. I'm not happy. I'm awful sorry."

"Sorry? Well, you have a fine way of showing it. You're just as bad as your sister, aren't you?"

"Mom, leave Daphne out of this."

"I will not." Mrs. Larrs looked me up and down. "You're crazy like your sister, aren't you? It runs in the family, doesn't it? You're just as mean as—"

I had never talked back to a grown-up before; now I couldn't stop myself. "My sister doesn't have a mean bone in her body!" I said, getting louder with each word. "But you—you, Mrs. Larrs—are a whole *heap* of mean! You say *mean, cruel* things. You hurt people's feelings on purpose!"

Elden smiled, giving me a thumbs-up sign.

"My sister is the kindest, most loving person I know. Any mean thing she has ever done has only been because she doesn't know any better!"

I grabbed my wrap and mittens, shaking. "And if you were so worried about my sister the other day, you should have kept a better eye on your baby!"

As I stomped out the door, I turned to look back. Mrs. Larrs was standing still as stone, and Elden kept right on smiling.

29

"You're kidding," Pop said, putting down his cup of cowpoke coffee. "You said *that* to Mrs. Larrs?"

I nodded, still shaking inside. I couldn't believe I'd spoken up that way all because of my sister.

"Well, knock me over with a feather!" Pop scratched his head. "And what did she say to you?"

"Nothing," I said. "Not one little word."

Mom giggled. Then Pop laughed. And before I knew it, we were all holding our sides, laughing.

"I know I shouldn't laugh," Mom said, "but I sure wish I could have seen her face."

"You can! Tomorrow! Please? Can't we go to the Christmas Tree Celebration? I'm just dying to hear Violet sing the solo."

Mom looked at Pop.

I turned to Daphne. "They'll be giving out goodie bags with candy and nuts. Want some candy?"

"Can-dee! Can-dee!"

I turned to Pop. "Please, Pop? Can't we go?"

Pop looked at Mom.

"Can-dee! Can-dee!"

"Please? Please?"

"Oh, all right, Ruthie bird. We'll go. I guess if you can stand up to Mrs. Larrs the way you just did, we don't have to worry so much about you."

Christmas Eve day we didn't have school, so I had no way of letting Violet know I would be at the celebration and decided to just surprise her.

All day long, I could hardly wait. I zipped through my chores, thinking of nothing else. I counted the chimes on the grandfather clock. I looked out the windows, praying for it to get dark.

Just when I was about to go out of my mind, the clock chimed six o'clock, and I dashed to my room. I fingered through my dresses—the ugly brown tweed, the plain black skirt, the blue paisley with the itchy lace collar, the green-checked flannel, which was almost threadbare, and the nice rose frock trimmed in white.

I decided on my rose frock with the garnet pin and bracelet Grandma gave me before she died. Grandma had said, "A jewel for a jewel." And tonight I felt like one.

I snuck into Mom and Pop's room and squirted on some of Mom's Midnight Passion perfume. I hardly ever wore perfume, except for weddings and funerals, but I guessed tonight's celebration qualified as a perfume occasion.

Then I stood in front of the hall mirror, combing and pulling and pinning my hair into a French twist like the ones the models wore in *The Saturday Evening Post*.

"Oh, Ruthie!" Mom exclaimed. "You're going to be the belle of the ball!"

Daphne put on her honey-gold dress with eyelet trim. Mom brushed her hair and waved it with the curling iron, making Daphne look like a fairy-tale princess.

Then Mom got all gussied up, too, in her red flannel with a blue collar and matching red hat.

"Woo-wee!" Pop said, looking at the three of us. "I'm with the best-lookin' gals in Kiowa County!"

"Are you sure you want to wear your hair up?" Mom asked as we bundled into the Tin Lizzy. "It's awful cold out here."

"I'm sure. Besides, I have my woolen wrap."

Mom's eyebrows knitted as she covered Daphne and me with a quilt. "Larry? Do you think we should risk this weather? Just look at this snow."

Pop gave Mom his "don't worry" look, and I scooted closer to Daphne as he drove into the icy darkness.

"Santa. Soft Santa."

"That's right," I told Daphne. "And he's going to give you a goodie bag filled with nuts and candy."

"Can-dee. Can-dee." Daphne pulled Josephine out from under our quilt and rubbed her only arm on my cheek. "Soft?"

"Mom?" I pinched my nose shut. "Does Daphne have to take Josephine?"

"Ruthie!" Mom turned around, frowning. "Mind your own business."

"It *is* my business. That dumb doll smells like stinky feet."

I shot Daphne a mean look.

She made one right back.

When we approached the hill before the schoolhouse, Pop turned our Lizzy around and started driving up backward.

"If these Lizzies were made the way they *should* have been—"

"—Henry Ford would have put the gasoline tanks under the *back* seat, instead of the front," I finished for Pop. He'd said that a million times.

Going uphill backward was usually fun, especially during the day. I always tried to see how close to the top we could get before I had to look. But tonight wasn't fun. Not only was it impossible for Pop to see, but he could barely keep on the road for all the ice and snow.

I squeezed Daphne's hand and closed my eyes.

"Soft. Santa soft?"

"Yes. Santa's soft."

Mom tapped her fingers on the dashboard. "Maybe we should go back home."

"Not on your life!" Pop said, topping the hill and turning our Lizzy around.

"Larry, this snow is only going to get deeper. Let's go back home."

Home? We were almost there. I held my breath and crossed my fingers.

"Don't worry, Ella Bess. I'll drain the radiator so it won't freeze. We'll be okay."

In a few minutes, we skidded into the schoolyard.

Despite the heavy snow, autos were parked everywhere—Tin Lizzies, Buick 6s, Hudson 37s, and even a fancy Brewster-Ford Town Car, with a crowd of admiring boys circled about it. I looked for Elden's tall head poking above the group, but didn't see it.

Daphne's eyes lit up at the sight of all the autos. She began counting them: "One, two, three, four, five . . ."

"Mom? Does she have to take Josephine?"

"Mind your manners, Ruthie."

And we got in line with everyone else, shivering in the icy wind—me, Mom, Pop, Daphne, and stinky old Josephine.

30

"Hey, look what the cat drug up!" a voice said behind me. I knew who it was, and my heart raced.

Baby Elizabeth was thrown over his shoulder like a sack of potatoes. She was all zipped up in a fuzzy pink snowsuit and bonnet, sucking on her tiny fingers.

"I thought you were inside, getting ready for the play," I said, suddenly feeling nervous. I started to reach for my hair, then realized what I was doing and stopped.

"Nope." Elden shifted Elizabeth to his other shoulder. "We just got here. Our Hudson slid into a ditch, and I had to get out and push."

Mom tweaked Elizabeth's nose. "How's baby Elizabeth?"

"Oh, she's dandy. Still cries up a storm, but that's the way she is. Don't worry, Mrs. T. She'll be fine." And he shoved his way through the line and disappeared into the school-house.

Mom looked at me oddly. " '*Mrs. T*'?"

Pop and I laughed.

Inside, the smell of turpentine lingered in the air. A box filled with empty paint cans and rags stood in the far corner. The stove door was open. Coals were burning bright red, but they couldn't keep up with the freezing wind, which burst in with every family that entered.

"Merry Christmas, Roger. Hello, Frank." Pop shook hands with all the menfolk. Mom beamed at all the ladies, even Mrs. Larrs.

"Mr. and Mrs. Tillman!" Miss Holman rushed over to shake their hands. She looked elegant in her black frock, bobbed hair, and pearl necklace. "I'm so glad you could make it. And would you look at Ruth Ann and Daphne! Why, they're pretty as can be."

I glanced around the room. Up onstage was a curtain. It wasn't a real curtain, just two white bedsheets sewn together with red felt stars glued all over them. Violet's head popped out, her neck all red and blotchy. "Ruthie!"

I made my way through the crowd.

"I'm so glad you came! I feel faint."

"Relax, Vi. Take some deep breaths. Say, shouldn't you be in your donkey costume?"

Violet's eyes filled with tears. Her neck turned even blotchier. "I can't find it!"

"Can't *find* it? Where did you see it last?"

"Elden had it."

"Elden?"

"He wanted to try it on. But I haven't seen him since."

Maybelle walked by in her Virgin Mary costume, acting surprised to see me. "Ruthie? What are you doing here?" She didn't give me time to answer. "You didn't bring Daphne, did you?"

"What business is it of yours?" I asked.

"Well, if you did, keep an eye on her. My two-year-old cousin, Sammy, is in the audience, and I wouldn't want her to . . . well, you know."

I gave her my coldest stare. "Come on, Vi. Let's go find Elden."

"There he is!" Violet said. "Hey, Elden! Where's my costume?"

"I gave it to Clayton."

"Clayton?"

"Don't worry, Vi. I'll find him. You sit down. Take some deep breaths and relax."

As I walked past Maybelle, I noticed that the back of her gown wasn't buttoned. The top button was, but the rest were gaping wide open for all the world to see.

Of course, I did the only decent thing a girl in my position could do—I didn't tell her.

31

There were so many people, it was impossible to find four seats together. So Mom and Pop scouted out two seats in the middle row for Daphne and me, then took two seats in the back row for themselves.

"Make sure she keeps her coat on," Mom instructed.

". . . twenty-one, twenty-two, twenty-three . . ." Daphne was in heaven, counting everything and everyone in sight.

"Stop counting!" I shoved Josephine under her coat. "It's not polite to point."

". . . twenty-four, twenty-five, twenty-six . . ." Daphne went right on counting people and shoes and hats. I pretended I didn't know her.

Someone tapped me on the shoulder.

"Here." Elden shoved a tiny green box tied with a red ribbon into my hand. "It's for, um, Christmas."

"Kiss-mus. Kiss-mus."

"Shh." I covered Daphne's mouth.

Elden looked up at the ceiling, down at the floor, then at me. "So, um, what did you do to your hair?"

"It's called a French twist. Do you like it?"

"Heck, yeah. You look pretty as a poinsettia." He sniffed the air. "You wearin' perfume?"

I nodded.

"Smells good!" Elden raised his eyebrows up and down several times. "Well, uh, Merry Christmas, Ruthie. Merry Christmas, Daphne."

"Merry Christmas to you, too."

He made his way to the stage. I looked at the tiny green box with its red ribbon. Part of me wanted to rip it right open and find out what it was. I'd never gotten a present from a boy before. But I put it in the pocket of my woolen wrap for later, when I would be all alone, with no sister to embarrass me.

Miss Holman stepped out from behind the curtain, rapping on a glass with a spoon. "May I have your attention, please? . . . We are about to begin, and I want to thank all the brave men who drove through ice and snow to get here tonight."

The men whistled and hooted.

"As you can see, School District 42 has worked very hard getting ready for this evening's celebration. So, without further ado, let's begin."

The curtain opened, and there stood the tallest, most elegant Christmas tree I'd ever seen, even nicer than Elden's. It was covered in flickering white candles, silver tinsel, a green garland, and brass bells. On top was a redheaded angel with wings made of peacock feathers, looking as if she had flown straight down from heaven and landed on our tree.

Daphne stopped counting long enough to say "Oooh" with everyone else, then continued, "Five, six, seven. Seven windows!"

"That's right. Now hush."

"One, two." She pointed to the door we came through and the door up onstage, which opened into the coal closet. "Two doors! Two doors!"

"Yes, Daphne. There are two doors. One. Two. Now stop pointing and be quiet."

Miss Holman began playing the piano, and out walked the Virgin Mary and Joseph. Maybelle had a pillow under her gown, making her look as if she was expecting. Marvin had a pretend mustache and beard made out of coffee grounds and maple syrup. He took Maybelle's hand and led her from inn to inn, where each innkeeper said the same thing: "Sorry. No room at the inn."

At first, no one seemed to notice the back of Maybelle's gown. But soon it was gaping wide open, and Marvin started snickering. Then the camel and sheep snickered, and before too long, even the audience began whispering.

Poor Maybelle. When I couldn't stand it any longer, I made my way up the side aisle and behind the curtain.

"Pssst!" I said, trying to get her attention. "Maybelle! You're unbuttoned!"

Maybelle turned every shade of red and came running toward me.

"Here, let me button you up," I whispered. "There you go." Then I made my way back to my seat.

Violet hee-hawed right on cue and in costume, too. The dancing snowflakes twirled and fluttered, and even though Ruby didn't wear her glasses, she didn't knock into anything.

Elizabeth looked like a real, honest-to-goodness baby Jesus, wrapped in a white towel. She played the part well, until the camel got too close to her manger. Then out it came—one of her bloodcurdling screams, loud enough to shake the windows.

"Baby cry!" Daphne shouted, covering her ears. "Cry loud!"

"It's all right." I grabbed her hand. "She'll stop in a minute."

But Elizabeth didn't. And before I knew it, Daphne was crawling under her seat, holding her ears.

Finally, Mrs. Larrs went up onstage and quieted down Elizabeth. Then Daphne came out of hiding.

Soon the play was over and it was time for the solo—my solo, which now belonged to Violet.

Violet waltzed out in the blue velvet dress, looking like a postcard. She had on new black patent-leather shoes, and her hair was pinned up into tiny curls fringing her face, making her look just like LeNora. I was so proud, I almost cried.

Miss Holman played the piano, making each key tinkle like lacy snowflakes falling from the sky.

Ruby and Clyde fluttered and twirled. Then Violet looked into the audience, and her face turned green as a gourd.

Come on, Vi. You can do it.

Our eyes met. I smiled and held up my pinky.

She smiled back, then closed her eyes and sang the prettiest version of "Silent Night" I'd ever heard.

32

During intermission, as folks were mingling over hot apple cider and mincemeat pies, Daphne wanted to go up onstage and see baby Elizabeth.

"No, Daphne. You stay with me."

"Baby soft. Soft."

"Yes. But she cries real loud, remember?"

Daphne covered her ears and looked frightened.

"Come on, let's go get some pie."

As we got in line, I noticed that someone had tied a big clump of mistletoe right over the pie table. All the menfolk were nudging each other and smiling at the ladies.

"How's the play so far?" Elden smiled his chipped-tooth smile.

"It's a doozy!" My cheeks flushed. Elden looked almost handsome in his purple Wise Man robe.

He looked at the ceiling. "Um, did you open my present yet?"

I fingered the box in my pocket. "Not in front of You-know-who."

"Know who. Know who."

"Well, you're gonna like what I got ya. Guess I better get back up onstage. See ya later, gator."

When all the mincemeat pies were eaten and the cider jugs emptied, everyone meandered back to their seats.

The curtain opened, and out walked Marvin Tallchief, shaking his fat belly. "Ho, ho, ho!" He made a grand Santa Claus, much better than last year's.

Last year no one had tried out for the part, so little Howard Sulkey volunteered. No matter how much stuffing we added, poor Howard looked more like a scrawny elf than a fat Santa.

"Santa! Santa!" Daphne stood up on her chair.

"Get back down." I pulled the hem of her coat, feeling everyone's eyes on us.

"Santa soft!" Daphne waved her arms as if she was flagging down the Rock Island.

I looked behind us to see what Mom and Pop wanted me to do. Mom was covering her face, and Pop just shrugged, mouthing, "Let her be."

How embarrassing.

Santa handed out several red goodie sacks. Then he reached under the tree to get another armload and knocked over a candle. Almost instantly, the tree was ablaze.

At first, folks laughed and joked.

"Attaboy, Santa!"

"Let's see some fireworks!"

"Here's the *real* show!"

But Marvin wasn't laughing. He grabbed a chair and began beating the tree. Elden took off his purple robe and tried to smother the flames, but in a matter of seconds, the flames reached the makeshift curtain and spread over each side of the stage, framing it in fire.

Screams and cries filled the schoolhouse.

Before I could blink, the kerosene lamps on each side of the room exploded into shooting fireballs. The Christmas tree fell into the audience, catching everything and everyone in its path on fire.

My first thought was of the drafty old window next to our seats. I lifted the bottom sash, but the steel netting that the school board had nailed on wouldn't budge.

I pounded it with my fist.

The man sitting next to me tried to kick it with his heavy boot.

People were throwing desks and chairs at the windows, but the steel netting that kept vandals out, kept us *in*.

A man on the other side of the room managed to climb through a torn corner of the steel netting. Frantic mothers passed their toddlers and babies to him.

Pastor BoJo stood on a desk, shouting with all his might, "Stay calm! Stay calm! God will see us through!" But staying calm was the last thing on our minds.

Smoke filled the room and rose in billowing clouds. In the panic of arms and legs, Daphne disappeared.

"Daphne!" I screamed. "Daphne!"

I fell to the floor, crawling between feet. "Daphne!"

But there were too many screams, too many people shoving and pushing, crawling on my back, climbing over my head, knocking me to the floor. *Oh, God, please help me. Please help us all.*

"Women and children first!"

"One at a time!"

The schoolhouse door opened inward, but the frenzied crowd *pushed* rather than *pulled*, and the door wouldn't open.

"Step back, everyone!"

"Don't panic. Don't push!"

Black smoke made it hard to see, hard to breathe. Flames were all around me.

Something heavy landed on my back, stomping me into the floor. Something else crushed my fingers—shoes—other people's shoes. I opened my mouth to call for Daphne, but no sound came, only a silent scream.

33

"Stand back!" a voice shouted. "Give her room to breathe!"

"Breathe, Ruthie. Breathe."

I tried to lift my head, but it weighed a ton. I opened my eyes. Cold air stung them, and I couldn't see.

"That's my Ruthie bird. Breathe nice and deep."

Pop's face—there were two of them—slowly came into focus.

People were hunched all around me, their faces smudged and mapped with tears. I was outside. *How did I get out here?*

"Mom! Pop!" A rush of cold air filled my lungs. I could barely swallow. "Wh-where's Daphne?"

"Shh," Mom said, brushing hair from my eyes. "Breathe, Ruthie. Don't talk."

People were crying, hugging, and swooning. The schoolhouse lit up the night, flames reaching in all directions.

Tires on the autos parked closest to the schoolhouse had melted into black gooey gobs. Windshields had cracked. Upholstered seats were in flames. Gasoline tanks had exploded, shooting flames into the already lit-up sky.

Pop ran to the pile of people clogging up the doorway to the burning schoolhouse. Ol' Man Rhemmer lay half in, half out, but no one could get close enough to save him. The fire was too intense.

Mom held my head in her lap, stroking my cheeks. "That's my girl. Breathe deep." She dug under the soot for a handful of white, clean snow and put it into my mouth. It was so cold, so wet, I choked, but it felt good on my throbbing throat.

The nine o'clock Rock Island came rattling down its tracks. The engineer's head was hanging out the window. He blew his train whistle to signal an alarm—unrelenting, like a high-pitched scream—as he chugged down the tracks toward Hobart.

Mom and I sat in the snow, staring, as the schoolhouse roof caved in and the walls collapsed, and the pungent smells of burning hair and gasoline filled the night sky.

"Where's Pop?"

"Shh," Mom said, pushing my swollen hands and fingers into the snow. "He and some of the men are searching for Daphne and the others."

"Daphne? The others? We've got to find them!"

"You're not going anywhere," Mom said, putting her hands on my shoulders.

"But Daphne—" I tried to stand.

Mom pulled me back down into the snow, and as I fell beside her, something soft dropped from my coat and brushed against my leg.

Josephine.

34

It took three hours for the Hobart firetrucks to get through the snow-packed roads to School District 42. By the time they got there, our beautiful one-room schoolhouse, with its freshly painted walls and spruce trimmings, was a charred skeleton.

People wailed and wandered about aimlessly, calling the names of their loved ones. Families huddled together, holding each other, crying. Prayers filled the blackened night, along with screams, shouts, and the question: *Why? Why did this happen?*

Pop carried me to our Tin Lizzy and slid me into the backseat. In a few minutes, he brought others—a man I didn't know, with flesh dangling from his hands, Mrs. Tallchief, her face all bloody, and Clyde Bushyhead's little brother, Raymond, with his foot badly burned.

Mom helped everyone get in, then rocked Raymond on

her lap as Pop cranked the engine and filled the radiator with snow.

"Daphne," I said. "Where's Daphne?"

Mom turned around in the front seat, tears filling her eyes. "Mrs. Rader said her husband took a load of injured to the Hobart hospital. So did Jim Sulkey and Frank McBee."

I struggled to speak. "Was sh-she one of them?"

"We hope so."

When our Lizzy rumbled to a start, Pop hopped inside, and we slid into the dark night.

"That's Frank McBee's Buick," Pop said. Our Lizzy skidded to a stop, then backed up to an auto stalled on the side of the road.

Frank McBee stood in front of his opened hood with smoke pouring out. "I forgot to put water back into my radiator!" he shouted. "It's so overheated, I can't get the cap off!"

Pop and Mom jumped from our auto and ran to the Buick, looking for Daphne. I tried to follow, but my hands wouldn't open the car door. They were all red, swollen twice their size, and they hung on the ends of my arms as if they didn't belong to me.

In a few minutes, Mom crawled back into our Lizzy, crying. Without even asking, I knew Daphne wasn't in Mr. McBee's auto.

Pop threw handfuls of snow onto the hot radiator and pried off its fire-hot cap with a rag. Then he and Mr. McBee scooped snow into the smoking radiator, jumping back as it sizzled and steamed.

"It's no use!" Mr. McBee finally shouted above his engine's sputtering. "Just go, Larry! Tell the hospital to send an ambulance!"

"Try it again!" Pop ordered. "Again!"

But the Buick refused to start.

"Go on!" Mr. McBee shoved Pop toward our Lizzy. "Get an ambulance! Hurry!"

Pop hopped back inside the auto and we sped off down the road, leaving the Buick and its injured passengers stranded in total darkness.

The Physicians and Surgeons hospital in Hobart had electric lights that poured out the windows, lighting up the parking lot like a heavenly refuge.

Autos were everywhere. People were everywhere. Three men in white jackets ran out to our auto. They quickly inspected each passenger, and rushed us into the hospital on skinny beds with wheels.

The hospital was so crowded, there was no place to put us. I ended up in the basement hallway. Before I knew what was happening, a nurse lifted me onto a cot. "Here, this'll help," she said, and she pushed my hands into a plastic tub of cool water.

My hands throbbed so badly, I screamed.

"It's all right, honey. Looks like you've got a few broken fingers. Stay here and we'll be with you as soon as we can, but meanwhile you're going to have to keep your hands in cool water." She pushed my hands back into the tub and hurried down the hall.

My head throbbed. My elbows ached. My chest was so sore, it hurt to breathe. The water turned pink, then red. I felt woozy, as if I was dreaming. Or was I fainting?

Up and down the hall were weeping, wailing people. Cots. Faces. Doctors. Bloody bandages. Nurses pushing blankets and sheets on carts that squeaked as they rolled by.

Where's Mom? Where's Pop? Daphne!

The room was spinning.

Squeak. Squeak. Another cart rolled by, this one covered with gauze, sponges, and towels.

"Ruthie. Ruthie, it's me."

I looked up into Elden's blackened face. The top of his hair was gone, clear to his scalp; so were his eyebrows and eyelashes. His nose was blistered and bloody.

"You all right?"

I opened my mouth, but nothing came out.

"Have you seen Elizabeth?" His voice sounded panicky, and tears flowed down his cheeks like little black rivers.

I shook my head, the room shaking with me. And when things came back into focus, Elden was gone and Mom was sitting beside me.

35

As the first ray of sun dawned on Christmas morning, almost everyone in Babbs Switch who wasn't in the hospital had gathered in the Hobart City Hall to identify the bodies.

Mom, Pop, and I made our way through the packed crowd. I clutched Josephine to my chest, though my hands were bandaged and throbbing.

Groups of people huddled here and there—by the windows, in corners, on the steps, in the hall—weeping, crying, holding one another up.

All around us, the smell of singed hair and burnt flesh lingered on our hair and coats. I hoped I'd be able to get it out of my wrap.

I scanned the crowd, searching for Daphne. I could barely whisper, but I asked and asked. No one had seen her. I asked about Violet, too. No one knew. Mrs. Suttner said she'd heard from Mr. Bushyhead that Violet's dad had been burned badly, but she didn't say anything about Violet.

The bodies were laid out in the back rooms, covered in white sheets. Only one person from each family was allowed to go see them. The rest of us had to sit in the lobby, waiting and wondering.

More and more people filed into the lobby, carrying dental records and photographs and scraps of material in hopes of matching them to the badly burned bodies.

One man was identified by his belt buckle. Another, by his boots.

Waiting was torture. Screams reminded us that at any minute our hopes could be crushed just as someone else's had been.

When our turn came, Pop went in alone. I tried to go with him, but the doors were slammed between us.

"We still haven't found Elizabeth," a shaky voice said.

I turned around.

Elden's hands trembled; his eyes were swollen from crying.

"I'm so sorry." I stumbled for words. "Where's your mom and dad?"

"In there." He pointed to a side door. "Mom went hysterical when Dad came out of the back rooms and said he couldn't find Elizabeth. She started screaming and shaking, so the doctor gave her something to settle her nerves."

He wiped his face, smearing soot from his cheek to his

nose and onto his coat. "All we found is this." He held up Elizabeth's tiny bonnet, unharmed by the fire.

I remembered that bonnet and how sweet Elizabeth had looked last night in her fuzzy pink snowsuit, thrown over Elden's shoulder like a sack of potatoes. Tears filled my eyes, and I wrapped my arms around Elden's neck, and we stood there crying for our sisters.

———

"It's amazing anyone got out of that fire alive," Miss Willowbright said, patting Mom on the back.

Mom didn't answer.

"All those people and only one door," Miss Willowbright continued. "Only one door."

The words "only one door" resounded in my brain like a big kettle drum. *Only one door.* Something about that bothered me, making me shiver. *Only one door.* Then I jumped to my feet.

"Mom! There were *two* doors! You know how Daphne's always counting? She counted *two* doors—the one we came through and the one onstage that went into the coal closet!"

Mom and Miss Willowbright gazed at me as if I'd lost my senses.

"Two doors! Two doors! Don't you see? Maybe Daphne went through the door of the coal closet!"

"Ruthie, if Daphne had gone into the coal closet, she wouldn't have been able to get out."

"But there's a chute. Don't you see? The coal is shoveled

from outside, then it slides down the chute, into the closet!"

Mom's face showed no emotion. Neither did Miss Willowbright's.

"Maybe Daphne went into the closet, then crawled outside through the chute!"

Mom lifted my hand and held it to her cheek. "I don't think Daphne could climb up a coal chute, Ruthie. She wouldn't even know what it was, much less that it led to outside."

"But what if she *did*?"

"Then why didn't she find us? Why didn't she answer us when we called? We searched all night long." Mom's eyes closed, and her head rolled from side to side as if she might faint. "We'd better accept it, Ruthie. Daphne's back there— right now—under one of those sheets."

"No!" I shook Mom's shoulders. "How can you even say that? She's alive! We've got to find her!"

I ran to the doors that separated the living from the dead. "Let me in!" I shouted, banging with my bandaged hands. "Open up!"

One door opened, and a little pipsqueak of a man in a white jacket appeared. "I'm sorry, but no children are allowed."

"I need to see my father."

"You'll have to wait. No one under twenty-one can enter these doors."

With a burst of energy and strength I didn't know I had, I pushed the man with my shoulder and ran into the long hall. "Pop! Pop! Come quick!"

Pop rushed out from one of the doorways, his face gray and lifeless. "What are you doing back here?"

"There were *two* doors! Daphne counted *two*! She escaped, don't you see? Through the door to the coal closet!"

The pipsqueak man in the white jacket grabbed my arm and started pulling me toward the door. "I said, no one under twenty-one behind these doors!"

"Wait!" I twisted from his grip. "I have to tell my father something!"

"No children allowed!"

Pop stepped between the man and me. "I believe my daughter has a right to speak. Go ahead, Ruthie bird."

"Daphne could have escaped through the coal closet!"

"The coal closet is gone," Pop said. "Burned to the ground with the rest of the schoolhouse."

"But she could have crawled up the coal chute! She could have gotten *out*!"

Pop stood there, his blistered hands on my shoulders, his blackened face staring into mine. "Was that chute big enough for Daphne to crawl through?"

"I don't know."

"Well, there's one thing *I* know," Pop said. "Daphne's not back here."

The doors slammed behind us as we stepped into the lobby. Pop's nostrils flared, his hands trembled. "Let's get Mom. We're going back to the schoolhouse."

"Wait!" Elden shouted. "I'm coming with you!"

36

Our Lizzy skidded to a halt in front of the smoldering pile of ashes. Shards of blackened boards lay strewn about. Curls of gray smoke rose high into the air, like kites on a windy day.

A dozen or so people were climbing through the debris, pulling up boards and emptying buckets of ashes. Three little boys ran by, playing tag, their faces covered in soot. "You're it!" one shouted. Two women were holding each other up, crying. One of them was Mrs. Sulkey.

"My Howie! He's gone!" she said. "My little genius!"

I stopped in my tracks. It couldn't be. Little Howard Sulkey? The boy with a million questions?

"Oh, I'm so sorry," Mom said. "We still haven't found Daphne!"

"Or my sister, Elizabeth!"

"You'll find them," Mrs. Sulkey said, shaking her head. "Just like I found my Howie—dead and gone!"

I ran to where the coal closet had been and rummaged through the debris: ashes; black, gritty snow; charred wood; the back cover from our dictionary, with the X, Y, and Z pages still attached; about one inch of a ruler; and a singed baby bootie.

"Elden!" I shouted. "Elden!"

Everyone came running.

Elden's eyes grew big. Then he whispered, in a voice so quiet I could barely hear, "Where did you find that?"

"Right here." I pointed to the spot. "Where did you find her bonnet?"

"Onstage, where the manger was."

"Fires do strange things," Mom said. "Lord knows, we'll probably find all sorts of oddities and not be able to explain them."

Pop rubbed his chin, thinking out loud. "Her bonnet was found over there." He pointed to the stage area. "And her bootie right here. Could she have crawled?"

"Nope." Elden shook his head. "She ain't big enough to crawl."

Just then, Hank and Hal Rutledge pulled up in their mother's Buick, honking. They ran toward us and shook hands with Pop. "We heard you couldn't find Daphne and baby Elizabeth. We've come to help look."

Pop's eyes filled with tears. So did mine.

"There's more comin', too," said Hank.

In a matter of minutes, five autos pulled up, organizing a thirteen-person search team, including Mr. and Mrs. Larrs.

Mrs. Larrs looked at me with teary eyes. "Ruthie," she said, "I've been thinking about what you told me the other day."

Me and my big mouth! Oh, why did I have to go and tell her off?

"And you are perfectly right!"

"I am?"

She nodded. "I *have* been cruel. Will you ever forgive me for all the awful things I've said?"

I looked at Mr. Larrs. Tears ran down his cheeks.

"Sure," I said. "Sure I'll forgive you."

Then we broke up into teams, searching in every direction.

37

After Elden and I had spent two hours searching in the icy cold, my bandaged hands ached clear to my elbows. My toes were so numb, they felt as though they'd fallen right off into my boots. My nose dripped, and I shivered so badly that I didn't think I could take even one more step without turning into a block of ice.

Every few minutes, Elden shouted, "Daphne! Elizabeth!"

But no answer came.

We trudged on, toward the empty train depot and along the railroad tracks, which were covered with snow and ice.

Walking along, I went over in my head all the places Elden and I had already searched. Elk Creek. Ditches. The woods. The school's cistern and outhouse and every outhouse, barn, and chicken coop we had passed.

The depot was my last hope. It was the only place we hadn't looked.

When it came into view, I started running like a frozen-stiff soldier. "Daphne!" I called, searching for footprints in the snow. "Daphne! Elizabeth!"

Elden slid open the door of the depot. I covered my eyes, afraid to look.

"Well? Are they in there?"

But I knew they weren't.

I lay down on the wooden floor, too tired, too cold, too disappointed to move another inch. Tears flowed like a water pump.

Elden sat down next to me, not saying a word. He put his arms around me, and we cried together for the second time that day.

Finally, Elden spoke. "Do you think we'll find them?"

"Sure." But the only thing I was sure about was that we'd looked in every place imaginable.

"Think, Ruthie. Where would you go if you were Daphne?"

My brain felt frozen. "I don't know. I just don't know."

"There's one place we still haven't looked."

"Where?"

"The hospital."

Elden was right. Maybe more people had been brought in since last night. What if Daphne was there, needing me, calling me? I stood up to go.

"Wait a minute. Sit back down here."

My heart raced, and words spilled out before I could catch them. "I can't! For as long as I've been alive, it's been

Daphne by my side. We sleep together. We eat together. We fight together. We do *everything* together. Don't you see? I've got to find her!"

Elden unbuttoned his coat and wrapped it around me like a blanket. "Calm down, Ruthie. Now, you stay here. I'll go find the others and see if they've checked the hospital and tell 'em where you're at."

"But I can't let you go out there with no coat. You'll freeze!"

"It's not me I'm worried about, it's you. Let's see, I better build a fire."

He went out and, in a few minutes, returned with an armload of sticks he had gathered. He put them on the cinder blocks in the corner. Leaving the sliding door ajar, he lit a match from his pocket, but the wood was too wet to burn.

"You got anything that'll burn?" Elden asked, taking off his boots. He pulled out some newspaper and wadded it into balls. He unbuttoned his shirt, taking out the sports pages. Then he lifted up his undershirt and pulled out the whole Sunday section, crossword puzzle and all.

Our eyes met, we laughed, and for a tiny second I forgot how cold I was, how my hands throbbed clear to my shoulders, and how badly I needed my sister to be alive.

38

That night, I lay in bed. Alone. It was the first time in my life I could remember sleeping without Daphne by my side.

She didn't stand up in bed like the Statue of Liberty, or jump up and down, or tuck her gown into the waistband of her underpants. She didn't demand a kiss for each cheek, her forehead, and Josephine.

I tossed and turned, thinking about our search and how everyone had agreed not to get discouraged and to meet again in the morning.

I thought about Hank and Hal Rutledge, who surprised us by searching longer and harder than anyone on the team.

I thought about how Mom and Pop had picked me up at the depot, and about our trip to the hospital, where I finally found Violet.

She was standing in the hallway of the main entrance,

next to her father's cot. His legs were wrapped in bloody gauze and his eyes were closed.

"Oh, Vi!" I had said, hugging her like a bear. "I've been so worried about you. Are you all right? How's your dad?"

Violet flinched. "I'm fine, except for this broken rib." She unbuttoned her coat to show me the gauze wrapped all around her chest. "The doctor's talking to my mom right now. They're wanting to move Daddy to a hospital in Oklahoma City. He's burned really bad." Then she noticed my hands. "Heavens! Are *you* all right?"

I tried to act as if it was no big deal. "These? Just a few broken fingers and burns. That's all."

She held my hands and looked at me with her saddest eyes yet. "We're really lucky to be alive." Tears fell onto her coat. "Did you hear the news?"

My heart skipped a beat. "What news?"

"R. W. McBee and Marvin Tallchief are dead."

I swallowed hard. "So is Howard Sulkey."

Violet gasped. "I heard Miss Holman is dead, too."

"Are you sure?"

Violet nodded. "They identified her body by the pearl necklace she had on. Pastor BoJo is gone, too."

I stood there, shocked, unable to gather my thoughts. All these people—dead and gone—and I'd thought they'd be here forever.

"Vi, we can't find Daphne or Elizabeth Larrs. We've looked everywhere. Here. At City Hall. In all the debris. They're nowhere to be found."

"Oh, Ruthie. How awful."

"We've looked up and down Elk Creek and a mile in each direction. We don't know where else to look."

Violet covered her heart and sat down on the floor. "But what about the firemen and the rescue workers? Can't they find them?"

I knew what she was hinting at. "Daphne's not dead, Vi. And neither is Elizabeth."

Violet leaned her head against the wall. "So do you really . . . I mean . . . How do you know they're alive?"

"I can't explain it, Vi. But I've got this funny feeling. A way-down-in-my-bones feeling. And it's telling me Daphne might have escaped through the coal chute with Elizabeth. I know it's farfetched and—"

"My Lord!" Violet said.

"What?"

"The last thing I remember was the coal closet."

"What about it?"

"Well, it's kind of fuzzy, but I remember the door being opened during the fire."

"Was it Daphne? Did she have Elizabeth?"

"I don't know. There were so many people. Too much smoke."

I swallowed hard. "Think, Vi. What did you see?"

"I saw someone open the door to the coal closet." She rubbed her eyes as if that would help her memory. "That's all I saw, Ruthie. Do you think it was Daphne?"

"I'm sure of it."

But now, all alone, lying in bed, I wasn't sure of anything. And the only feeling I had way down in my bones was a dull, cold ache. I kicked the hot brick at the foot of our bed.

Dear God,

You're the only one who knows if Daphne and Elizabeth are alive. Please, make them be alive. And show me where they are . . .

You know, I really don't understand this. Why did you let so many good folks die? And Miss Holman, of all people. She was the best teacher in the entire world.

Is life just a game to you? Like one big checker-board? You move us from space to space and whatever happens, happens? Is life all a matter of luck and chance? Or do you have some sort of strategy that no one knows about?

I was too angry to say amen.

And I made Josephine's only hand count all sixty squares on our quilt.

39

I awoke in bed, startled.

Sitting up, I tried to calm my racing heart. My hands and fingers ached so badly, I couldn't help but cry.

I rubbed Josephine against my cheek. "Where is she, Josephine? Where's my sister?"

For the millionth time, I went over in my head all the places the search teams had looked. I thought about Elden's question: *If you were Daphne, where would you go?*

Where would I go? I pictured all the places between the schoolhouse and here. The depot. Elk Creek. The barns. The outhouses. The ditches. The chicken coops. Ol' Man Rhemmer's—

Oh my gosh! It couldn't be . . . it could *be!*

"Mom! Pop!" I ran to their bedroom. "I know where Daphne is! I know where she's at!"

Pop sat up in bed.

I tried to catch my breath. "Elden asked if I was Daphne where would I go, and I know where I'd go!"

"Where?" Mom asked.

"Ol' Man Rhemmer's haystack! Daphne and I stopped there a few weeks ago."

Mom and Pop stared at each other, their eyes all puffy from crying. "Are you sure she's there?"

"Yes. Well, no. I mean, I don't know! Let's go look!"

In a split second our Lizzy was rambling down the road, headlights shining in the darkness.

When we got close to the haystack, I could barely control myself. "Daphne!" I shouted out the window. "Daphne!"

We parked the Lizzy and stomped through the knee-deep snow, making our way toward the huge haystack with our lantern.

"Daphne!"

"Daphne!"

We scrambled over the barbed-wire fence.

"Daphne!" I rummaged through the hay. "Daphne!"

Hay flew from Mom's fingers. "Daphne! Are you in here?"

No answer.

Pop handed Mom the lantern, saying, "Here, let me search."

We searched and searched.

We called and called.

"It's no use," Mom said, crying. "We could search all night and not find her."

"I think we should go."

"No, wait! Let's look a little longer!"

"We already have, Ruthie bird. It's time to go."

"Daphne!" I shouted. "If you can hear me, do something!"

We watched for a sign. Nothing happened.

"Move your hand, Daphne! Move your foot! Show us where you're at!"

Mom put her arm around my shoulder. "Come on, Ruthie—"

"No! She's here! I just know it."

"But *where?*"

"Daphne!" I hollered. "We need your help! We can't find you without your help!"

We waited in silence.

"Come on, Ruthie bird. Let's head—"

"Did you hear that?"

"What?"

"I don't know, but I heard something."

"Ruthie, you're imagining things. Now, let's—"

"Wait! There it was again! A rustling noise." I held up the lantern. "Daphne?"

Another rustle.

"Daphne?"

And suddenly a hand popped out of the hay.

"My goodness gracious!"

"Daphne Sue!"

"You're alive!"

Pop carried Daphne to our Lizzy, and we all climbed in, unable to believe our eyes. Her lips were blue. Her face was white as snow. Her hands were cold as ice.

Mom wrapped her in our quilt.

"Fire. Fire. Hot."

"Daphne? Did you crawl up the coal chute?" I asked.

Daphne didn't answer.

"Baby. Soft, soft."

Mom and I looked at each other. "Do you know where baby Elizabeth is?" I asked.

Daphne hung her head. "Cry. Cry." She covered her ears, and out of her coat fell the white towel that had been Elizabeth's costume.

"Daphne Sue!"

"Where's Elizabeth?"

"Baby cry. Cry loud!"

I swallowed hard. "Do you know where she is?"

Daphne shook her head.

"Is she in the haystack?"

"No, no. Baby."

"Then where *is* she?"

Daphne only stared.

Pop cleared his throat. "Daphne Sue, you won't get in trouble. I promise. Now, where's Elizabeth? Where's the soft baby?"

She pointed to the haystack.

40

"Wait!" I ran after Pop, who had already hopped the barbed-wire fence. "Wait for me!"

Pop didn't wait. He ran like a madman into the night. "Elizabeth!" he shouted. "Elizabeth!"

In a few minutes, we were back at the haystack. Pop held up the lantern. "You know the chances of Elizabeth being alive are about one in a million. Are you sure you don't want to stay with Mom and Daphne?"

"Positive."

We searched through the hay, my hands aching clear to my shoulders.

I bit my lip. "Pop? What if Daphne squeezed her too tight? What if she killed Elizabeth just like Boots?"

"Daphne gets scared to death when Elizabeth cries, so I doubt that. Here, you hold the lantern."

"I can't!" I showed him my bandaged hands.

"Then I'll hold it and *you* climb in there."

"But what if I step on her?" My heart trembled at the thought.

"Then you'll step on her. We need to find her. Hurry!"

Pop held the lantern high as I climbed onto the haystack. Chunks of hay fell on top of me, covering my head.

I searched frantically.

"Do you feel anything?"

"I don't know! It's hard to feel with my hands bandaged!"

Pop was throwing hay all about. "She's got to be here. She's just *got* to be here. Somewhere. In all this hay . . . Oh, my gosh!"

"What?"

Pop was speechless.

I jumped down and ran to where he stood.

There lay baby Elizabeth, her lips blue and her skin icy white.

"Is—is she alive?"

"I don't know." He picked her up and held her small body against his chest. "Come on, Elizabeth. Come on, baby. Be alive!"

She didn't move. She didn't even open her eyes.

"Maybe she's asleep. Shake her a little."

Pop rocked her up and down. "Come on, Elizabeth." He put his hand in front of her nose, feeling for breath. "Breathe, Elizabeth. Breathe."

"Wake up, Elizabeth."

And out came a bloodcurdling scream.

41

"It's a miracle," Doc Bailey said, coming out of the examination room. "A downright miracle."

Mom and Pop and I still couldn't believe it. Elden and his parents sat next to us, tears streaming down their faces.

"My baby's alive! She's alive!" Mrs. Larrs said over and over. She put her arms around me, weeping. "Daphne saved my baby!"

Doc continued, "Looks like they both have some frostbite. We won't know for a while yet how serious it is."

"They'll—they'll be fine, won't they?" I asked.

Doc lifted his shoulders. "I think so. But we're going to have to keep a close eye on them, especially the baby." Doc looked at me real seriously. "Ruthie, if you hadn't found them when you did, they wouldn't have made it through the night."

Chills went up my back. "Can I go in to see my sister now?"

"Better let her sleep," Doc said. Then, to the rest of us, "I think you could *all* use some sleep. Why don't you go home and come back in the morning."

At the first crack of dawn, we rumbled our way back to the hospital, but we hadn't slept a wink—we were much too excited. Mom and Pop rushed in as soon as we got there.

Doc made me wait for my turn. "We can't have so many people in there at once."

Mom and Pop came out smiling. I went in.

Daphne's bed was in the corner, by the window. When she saw me, she grinned.

"I've got a surprise for you," I whispered, kissing her forehead.

Her eyes lit up.

"Shh . . . Don't tell anybody."

"Kitty! Kitty!" Cinnamon tumbled out of my pocket onto her bed.

"Both of his eyes are open now. See?"

"Kitty. Hold?"

I put her hands around Cinnamon's belly. "See? Be gentle. Don't squeeze."

Daphne's eyes gleamed. "Kitty soft!" She rubbed her cheek across his soft fur.

"I have another surprise for you."

"Can-dee? Can-dee?"

"Even better." And I pulled a freshly washed Josephine from under my wrap. "See her new arm? I made it out of a scrap from Mom's rag bag. See her new pigtails? They're made out of yarn. Doesn't Josephine look dandy?"

Daphne frowned.

"You don't like her new pigtails?"

She shook her head no. Yanking off the pigtails, she put them on Cinnamon's head, laughing. "Fun-ny. Fun-ny."

"Fun-ny," I agreed, and kissed my one-of-a-kind sister on her cheek, her other cheek, and her forehead. I even kissed Josephine.

42

The next day, a service was held for the dead. Hundreds of people packed into the Hobart City Auditorium, weeping and moaning for the people who'd lost their lives in the fire at School District 42.

A preacher from Lone Wolf silenced the crowd and opened with a solemn prayer: "And God shall wipe away all tears from their eyes; and there shall be no more death, neither sorrow, nor crying, neither shall there be any more pain: for the former things are passed away."

Nervously, I made my way up front.

"And now we have a song by a Babbs Switch student, Miss Ruth Ann Tillman."

I stood behind the pulpit, my heart racing, looking into the crowd. I searched through the teary-eyed faces, the heads, the hats. Then I found her—Daphne. We shared a smile, a smile that only sisters share, then "Heaven's Doors Are Opening" rolled off my tongue, sounding like a prayer.

———————————

At the Hobart Cemetery, twenty caskets sat waiting to be buried in a huge, single grave, forty feet long by seven feet wide. More were to be buried later.

"These are they which came out of great tribulation, and have washed their robes, and made them white in the blood of the lamb," the preacher said.

Then, one by one, all twenty caskets, white, black, and gray, were lowered into the huge hole in the frozen ground.

"There goes the best teacher that ever lived."

I turned around. Elden was dressed up in a gray suit and woolen coat, his face full of tears. "She taught me how to read and write."

"Me, too."

"She never paddled me. Even when I deserved it."

We watched as more caskets were lowered.

"There goes little Howard Sulkey."

"And Pastor BoJo." Elden wiped his nose on his sleeve. "He was a good man."

"He was the *best*."

"You know the last thing I heard Pastor BoJo say in the fire? He said, 'God will see us through.' "

"Do you think God will?"

"I dunno. We're here, aren't we?"

"Yes, but what about *them*?" Another casket went into the ground. "Why did God let them die?"

"I don't think He did. God didn't put candles on that Christmas tree."

"So you don't think there's a meaning to all this? Is life just a matter of luck and chance?"

"Heck, if I knew that, I'd be God."

I handed Elden my handkerchief, thinking about what he'd said.

He blew his nose, long and loud, then tried to give me the wet handkerchief.

"Um, that's okay, you keep it."

"No, *you* keep it."

"Really, I don't mind."

"Here."

I gave up. When I stuffed it back into my pocket, I felt the small green box with the red ribbon Elden had given me at the Christmas Tree Celebration.

"I guess I forgot to open this."

"Well go on, then. Open it."

"Here? At the burial?"

Elden grabbed the box, unwrapped it, and lifted the lid. Inside was a shiny gold tube of lipstick. He took off the top and rolled it out.

It was mushy and kind of lopsided from the fire, but there was no doubt about it—*Flamingo Pink!*

Elden smiled.

My heart pitter-pattered. "I've never had a tube of lipstick before. Thank you."

"When you become rich and famous, you can write in your autobiography that I gave you your first tube of lipstick."

My cheeks flushed. "And my first kiss." I looked around to see if anyone was listening. She was.

"Kiss. Kiss. Kiss-mus."

"Shh, Daphne. Be quiet."

"Well, I better go check on my family." Elden cupped my elbow in his hand. "See ya later, gator."

Daphne rubbed Josephine against my cheek. "Two arms. One, two. Two."

"Yes, two arms."

"Kitties. Tell me kitties."

"Here? Now?"

"Kitties!"

"Well, all right. We have two kittens."

"Green?"

"No, goose egg. Kittens don't come in green. Nutmeg is gray and Cinnamon is orange."

"Hold?"

"Yes," I said, "but only when I'm with you, and only if you remember to be gentle."

"Count. Count."

"That's a good idea, Daphne. Let's count together." We counted autos and people, hats and shoes. We counted caskets and babies and mittens. We even counted Stinky and

Pot Licker, who'd managed to find their way to the cemetery.

When the service was done, Maybelle and Violet came running over. "Did you hear the news?" Maybelle asked. Violet was beaming.

"What news?"

"There's two newspaper reporters looking for Daphne. They came all the way from New York! They're calling her the Haystack Hero!"

"A *hero*? Daphne Sue, did you hear that? You're a hero!"

"He-ro, He-ro."

"Ruthie?" Maybelle said, looking down at her shoes. "I'm really sorry for what I said about Daphne the other night. I didn't deserve for you to be so nice to me and button my gown during the play."

Now it was my turn to look down. "I owe you an apology, too."

"Whatever for?"

"I knew your gown was unbuttoned before the play even began."

Maybelle's face turned pale. Then she smiled and broke out laughing. "I guess I deserved that, didn't I? Apology accepted." She hugged Daphne and took her over to the reporter's flashing cameras.

"How are your hands?" Violet asked.

"They hurt. How's your rib?"

Violet grimaced, then smiled. "As long as I don't breathe, I'm all right."

"How's your father? Did they move him to Oklahoma City?"

Violet nodded. "He's going to have skin grafts on his legs and chest. The doctors say he'll be fine, but it'll take a long time to heal. Say, I have a present for you. Close your eyes and hold out your hand."

I did as I was told. When I opened them, I gasped. "Vi! Are you sure you want to give them to me?"

"Sure, I'm sure." Violet tied the silver ribbons on my braids. "There. What do you think?"

"I think you're the best friend a girl could ever have!"

She held out her pinky. "You know, Ruthie, it's going to be awfully hard to lock pinkies with all those bandages."

"How about this?" I offered up my elbow. "Friends till the cow jumps over the moon?"

"And the dish runs away with the spoon."

Then we locked elbows for the very first time.

Author's note

Although the characters in this story are fictional, the small town of Babbs Switch, Oklahoma, is real. It was a thriving community until a fire in its one-room schoolhouse claimed the lives of thirty-six people on Christmas Eve, 1924. Among the dead were sixteen students and their teacher.

Because of that fire, nationwide laws were enacted, restricting the use of candles on Christmas trees in public buildings and making sure that all public schools had more than one entrance, windows that were not obstructed in any way, and doors that opened outward rather than inward.

Babbs Switch, located a few miles south of Hobart in the Quartz Mountain area, is now a ghost town. All that is left of the town is a tiny park with two picnic tables where School District 42 once stood. A large granite marker states:

SITE OF BABBS SWITCH TRAGIC SCHOOL FIRE. On Dec. 24, 1924, 35 people lost their lives while attending a Christmas party in a one-room frame

school house. The fire was started by a candle on a
Christmas tree. A school building was built here as a
memorial and a model to point the way to safer county
schools the nation over. The school was discontinued in
1943, was dismantled and sold.

Although the marker states that thirty-five people lost their lives, a thirty-sixth person, a four-year-old girl, is assumed to have died in the fire. She disappeared that night and was never found.